EVERYMAN,
I WILL GO WITH THEE,
AND BE THY GUIDE,
IN THY MOST NEED
TO GO BY THY SIDE

ALEXANDER SOLZHENITSYN

ONE DAY IN THE LIFE OF IVAN DENISOVICH

TRANSLATED FROM THE RUSSIAN
BY H. T. WILLETTS

WITH AN INTRODUCTION
BY JOHN BAYLEY

EVERYMAN'S LIBRARY
Alfred A. Knopf NewYork London Toronto
219

THIS IS A BORZOI BOOK

PUBLISHED BY ALFRED A. KNOPF

First included in Everyman's Library, 1995
Originally published under the title *Odin den' Ivana Denisovicha* in
Novy Mir, Moscow, 1962
World Copyright © 1978 by Aleksandr Solzhenitsyn
English translation Copyright © 1991 by Farrar, Straus & Giroux, Inc.
and HarperCollins Publishers
Published in the US by arrangement with Farrar, Straus & Giroux, Inc.
and in the UK by arrangement with the Harvill Press.

Introduction, Bibliography and Chronology Copyright © 1995 by
Everyman's Library
Typography by Peter B. Willberg
Ninth printing (US)

US website: www.randomhouse.com/everymans

ISBN: 0-679-44464-5 (US)
1-85715-219-0 (UK)

A CIP catalogue reference for this book is available from the
British Library

Book design by Barbara de Wilde and Carol Devine Carson

Typeset in the UK by AccComputing, North Barrow, Somerset

Printed and bound in Germany by GGP Media GmbH, Pössneck

ONE DAY IN THE LIFE
OF IVAN DENISOVICH

———

INTRODUCTION

Many books have now been written about the Soviet labour camps. Thanks to Western Sovietologists, the term *Gulag* has become as familiar in the Western media as it once was in the enormous undercover society which populated the Soviet penal system, and formed an integral part of a vast but ramshackle command economy.

For years that immense area of suffering was muffled in a profound silence. Most if not all Russians knew what was happening; many had friends or relatives who had been snatched away into its underworld; but intimidation and censorship prevented any statement, whether in art or in journalism, of the scale of horrors actually in progress. During the war, and the lifetime of Stalin, Western apologists or enthusiasts for the Soviet Union also had some idea of what was going on; but the sheer scale of the system, and the savagery with which it was run, was ignored or whitewashed, until determined scholars like Robert Conquest embarked on comprehensive research. Even then, the findings revealed, however accurate and even understated, were often questioned, and alleged by committed socialists in all countries to be greatly exaggerated.

But there were Russian writers who had been in the Gulags, and who knew the facts. At the time of the first 'thaw', under Khrushchev in the early Sixties, cautious attempts were made in the Soviet establishment to reveal some part of what had taken place under Stalin. Of course this was not being done on humanitarian grounds, and certainly not with the intention to discredit the Soviet system, but as a tactical ploy to make the new government and its leaders popular, and earn them a degree of genuine support, as opposed to the idolatrous lip-service paid for years to Stalin. Nevertheless, the dismantling of a legend, once begun, was hard to halt.

One of the first beneficiaries was former artillery captain Alexander Solzhenitsyn, who, in the last year of the Great Patriotic War against Germany, had been arrested on the

North-Western front by the Soviet counter-intelligence organization SMERSH for writing disrespectful comments about Stalin in a letter to a fellow officer on another part of the front. In *The Gulag Archipelago*, also admirably translated by H. T. Willetts, Solzhenitsyn tells the nightmarish but farcical story of how this arrest took place, while German shells were falling a few yards away and senior artillery captain Solzhenitsyn was urgently needed to organize counter-battery work. But the needs of 'security' took preference over those of the battle, and Solzhenitsyn was carted off to Moscow by SMERSH, where he began his imprisonment by being required to show his escort how to find their way to the Lubianka gaol. He was not released until 1953, having experienced all the many varieties of camp life, and undergone the regime described in *One Day in the Life of Ivan Denisovich*.

He began writing the first drafts of the story after his return from exile, and the progressive editor of the magazine *Novy Mir* took the controversial step of deciding to try for publication. The timing could not have been more fortunate, as Khrushchev's reforms were just beginning, and this successor of Stalin is himself reported to have authorized the publication of a censored and watered-down version of the book in the influential periodical, the nearest thing to an avant garde publication that existed in the Soviet Union. The present text restores the cuts that were then made, and which had been accepted by Solzhenitsyn himself as the best way to get at least the gist of his tale, and its devastating significance, into print.

Solzhenitsyn was not the only writer from the camps to benefit in this way from the thaw. Varlam Shalamov, who spent many years in the far-eastern goldmining settlement at Kolyma, where conditions were even harsher than anything in Ivan Denisovich's experience, was now inspired by his example to produce his own stories of camp life, *Kolyma Tales*, which have also been translated into English. At one stage after their release Solzhenitsyn asked Shalamov to collaborate with him in the production of further books and reports about the Gulag, but the elder writer felt too ill and tired, after the hardships of his exile, to help with the project. None the less, his own book of stories, together with *One Day in the Life of*

INTRODUCTION

Ivan Denisovich, form twin classics of the Gulag. Both are works of art in an absolute sense, although Solzhenitsyn's masterpiece demonstrates the more perfect concentration of purpose, together with simplicity and economy of effect.

For the greatest strength of *Ivan Denisovich* is its exemplary force, its total commitment to a vital and heroic purpose. Russian speakers, readers of *Novy Mir*, were at once bowled over by the confidence, forcefulness and brilliance of its style, a wholly new amalgam of simple Russian narrative (Daniel Defoe's *Robinson Crusoe* affords us some sort of English parallel) blended with colloquialisms, pungent slang and prison-camp jargon, the whole giving that unmistakable impression of the *new* which is decisive in the authority of a literary masterpiece of this kind. Ordinary reportage about the real nature of the camp system would have had some effect on the reading public, of course; but the shock achieved by Solzhenitsyn was a literary shock as well as a social one. Literature had, as it were, abruptly come to terms with the unique horrors of this form of slave economy, and showed that it could master what it really signified, presenting graphically the kind of world on which the Soviet political philosophy ultimately rested.

The numerous and impressive imaginative works which Solzhenitsyn has produced since *Ivan Denisovich* have rightly won him an increasing fame. But it is to be wondered whether any of them are quite so decisively effectual in their artistic impact as *Ivan Denisovich*. His success led to the award of the Nobel Prize, which was of course for Western diplomats as much a move in the Cold War as a recognition of the author's superb achievement; the Soviet authorities retaliated by revoking Solzhenitsyn's Russian citizenship, and sending him into exile.

Until 1994 he lived in America, in Vermont; and although he returned to Russia after the collapse of the Soviet Union, with his citizenship restored, America had long been his seemingly permanent home. Like many other Soviet writers he found his world, his subject and philosophy of life increasingly left behind by the rapidity with which events were moving. Some exiles and protesters, whether outside or inside the former Soviet Union, were disposed by the change, though in an uncertain way, to support the revival of whole-hearted capitalism, together with the anarchy of ideas and ideals associated with the birthpangs of a new democracy. Solzhenitsyn was by no means one of these. His view of Russia and Russian government was old-fashioned and even autocratic, associated with the revival of the Orthodox Church, and of its former authority. It remains to be seen whether this vision of a future Russian society will have any appeal to his fellow citizens.

While living in America Solzhenitsyn had determined to make his great work a detailed examination of the root causes of the Soviet system, and the birth of the methods which it had always used, whether under Lenin or Stalin. Himself a highly efficient soldier who knew much about war, its techniques and logistics, he determined that the heart of the matter lay in those first disastrous campaigns of the Russian army in the first Great War, begun under the Tsar in 1914. A massive novel, *August 1914*, was the result; and it was further enlarged and elaborated into the later sequence which composed *The Red Wheel*.

There is something altogether admirable about Solzhenitsyn's obsession with discovering what went wrong in Russia, and devoting his great literary talents to an elaborate post-mortem. Yet it must also be admitted that *The Red Wheel* was, in a sense, out of date before it appeared, whereas *Ivan Denisovich* still has the air of changeless freshness – the shock of the present – which it had when it first broke upon the Russian public. It was news, and not history: and it retains the power that the latest news has to shock, surprise, and engross the reader. Its very simplicity is its most potent appeal, whereas its author's subsequent and scholarly reconstruction of the events and personalities that led to the 1917 revolution are bound to lack the same political immediacy. It is often said today that Russian dissident authors lost their subject overnight when the Soviet Union collapsed: but for dissident writers of real stature, like Solzhenitsyn and Andrei Bitov, the event was also a new challenge. They, and their successors, will infallibly find out the beginnings of that new life in their country which art can discover, and shed light upon.

This is because history is omnipresent in Russian literature, in a more urgent and overwhelming sense than in the case of other, perhaps more fortunate countries. History, and also servitude. Russian literature is full of prisons, and of those who have experienced imprisonment. In one of his poems the turn-of-the-century poet Maximilian Voloshin, one of the distinguished figures of Russia's 'Silver Age' of poetry, comments on the strange fondness of Russians for their grim tradition of slavery, exile and penal servitude. It is a tradition that, with prophetic foresight, the poet saw as surviving the coming of revolutionary 'freedom' and continuing in a new era in an even more exaggerated form. He guessed right, not that it was perhaps so hard to guess. And this servitude remained a dominant theme and nightmare in the Russian consciousness.

The great Russian novelists of the nineteenth century – Tolstoy and Dostoevsky especially – were well aware of the fact. Pierre in *War and Peace* is a prisoner of the French, and the sequence of his captivity in Moscow, and in the hardships of the French retreat, is one of the most memorable in the novel. The convicts of Tolstoy's last novel, *Resurrection*, are its most vivid and important characters. Chekhov's account of his journey to the prison settlement on Sakhalin Island, and of the prisoners and guards he found there, was more important to him, and to his vision of himself as a writer, than any of his stories and plays. Dostoevsky above all, in *The House of the Dead*, wrote out of his own days as a convict what is surely the most definitive account of the Russian prison experience.

So in what ways does Solzhenitsyn manage to add his word to the list of Russian masterpieces already written on this topic?

That is an interesting question. And it can perhaps best be answered by a brief quotation from the story itself. The chief character, Shukhov, is talking with his mates round the stove at the work-place, and the others are envying the fact that he has nearly done his time – ten years. Another convict is serving twenty-five.

In happier days everybody got a flat ten. But in '49 a new phase set in: everybody got twenty-five regardless. Ten you could just about do without turning up your toes. But twenty-five?

Shukhov enjoyed it. He liked people pointing at him – see that man? He's nearly done his time – but he didn't let himself get excited about it ... They could twist the law any way they liked. When your ten years were up they could say good, have another ten. Or pack you off to some Godforsaken place of exile.

'They could say good, have another ten.' It is that kind of casual colloquial sentence which makes its greatest impact in *Ivan Denisovich*. It is an effect, and a shock, quite unlike anything to be found in Tolstoy or Dostoevsky. In their writing about servitude some sort of rationale, and even of a rule of law, is taken for granted, no matter how harsh and tyrannical it may be. But the Gulag system is not run by men who have some notion of justice and propriety, however autocratic and misguided, but by gangsters. The state and its apparatus have been taken over by those who have responsibility to no one, and least of all to the system in which they profess to believe, and which is supposedly leading society on to the 'gleaming heights' of socialism.

The *zeks* in the camp are perfectly well aware of all this. As Solzhenitsyn remarked in his novel, *The First Circle*, the only sense of genuine freedom you could get in the Soviet Union was inside a labour camp. All so-called beliefs, and all hypocrisies, were left outside. The *zeks* well understood that they were in the power of men who simply did what they liked, and who on a whim might either release you, or re-imprison you. It is this sense of utter cynicism, underlying a whole stifling mass of pious ideology, that Solzhenitsyn conveys so casually and so economically. No doubt many of the readers of *Novy Mir* were themselves, and in their hearts, perfectly well aware of the fact. But to hear the truth spoken out with such unheard-of pungency and clarity! To see it written in print, and in the regime's most respected magazine, as if it were something well-known and taken for granted! That really was a surprise.

And yet it may be that the word 'cynicism' is out of place here. In so far as cynicism is a feature of Russian life (and Conrad, the great Polish novelist and hater of all things Russian, firmly stated it to be so) it has always been twinned, so to speak, with an equally unbounded idealism. Idealism of a spontaneous and not of an ideological kind. Solzhenitsyn as a young man was not only himself a passionate idealist, like most Russians, but was prepared to link that idealism with the programme and ideology of the Communist regime. He had become disillusioned early on, probably well before his arrest. But he remained an idealist none the less, even as a *zek* in a Gulag, even when he had lost the last shred of belief in the Revolution and in its aims.

This was partly because he was already finding, in the camps, evidence of the survival of religion, and the heroism of those men and women who had been imprisoned for their beliefs, or who had rediscovered them inside. Still more important, Solzhenitsyn's belief in human beings and their human individuality was vastly strengthened by his experiences. Shukhov and his fellows are not only clearly marked individuals but essentially men of good will; not in any priggish or pompous sense, but in their unconscious need to help themselves by helping each other; in their small pleasures, their jokes, their attempts to circumvent the guards and get round the regulations. In spite of his hatred of the Soviet system, and its utter moral bankruptcy, Solzhenitsyn takes a very 'positive' view of life, a view which is traditional to the hopefulness which Russian writers have always tended to show about Russia's future.

In spite of the horrors of the present, things will get better some time; and this will be due to the efforts and the good will of human beings themselves, and not to any ideology or system. In *The Oak and the Calf* Solzhenitsyn quotes those well-known lines of Pushkin which are also quoted more than once in Dostoevksy's *Diaries*. 'In hope of all the good and glory/I look ahead devoid of fear.' That is also the message of *Ivan Denisovich*; and it may go some way to explain why the editor of *Novy Mir*, and other more or less enlightened Soviet intellectuals who were themselves secretly disillusioned with the system, were able to take the line they did, when making the daring decision to publish Solzhenitsyn's story.

For the story still preaches that gospel of work and hope which was an integral part of the old idealism of Leninist Bolshevism, and which had actually formed the subject matter of so many dull Soviet novels. Even though none of the *zeks* has the faintest respect for the Soviet system, they are still all portrayed here as believers in work and comradeship; and in some cases, such as that of the Baptist, something more positively religious than that. In the camps, Solzhenitsyn, like Dostoevsky, discovered religious faith for himself, and later joined it to a traditional adherence to the Russian Orthodox church.

It is significant that no such hope for the future is to be found in the work of that other master of the literature of the Gulag – Varlam Shalamov. *Kolyma Tales* presents an unrelievedly terrible picture of camp life, in which the convicts murder each other without fear of discovery by the guards and the criminal elements prey upon the 'politicals' like wolves upon sheep. By contrast, there is an almost suspicious degree of law and order, and even something resembling 'boy scout's honour', in the camp society of *Ivan Denisovich*. No doubt the camps did vary very greatly in their kinds of organization and morale; but even so, it is illuminating to contrast the Shalamov stories, which of course were not published in Russia until long after *Ivan Denisovich*, with the description given by Solzhenitsyn.

Both writers share, none the less, a mastery of detail in their accounts of camp life, which is often chilling both in its matter-of-factness and in its lack of emphasis. Solzhenitsyn, for example, depicts the search of the convicts at the end of the day, before they are allowed back into the camp which is 'home' to them (the Russian word 'domoi' has a special domestic plangency). Shukhov is in terror in case the guard who searches him should discover the bit of broken blade he has managed to conceal in a work mitten; and the reader shares fully in his sense of utter relief when the searcher misses it. Discovery would have meant ten days in the 'hole', without soup, almost equivalent to a death sentence when the thermometer stands at nearly 30 degrees below. Another arrestingly casual detail reveals how the guards are trained never to approach close to convicts with gun in hand, not because they might be tempted to shoot – that would not have mattered – but because the convicts might manage by a concerted rush to wrest the weapon from them. The guards' policy must always be to divide and demoralize their charges, and prevent any attempt at communal action. On the all too rare occasions when such action did take place, as recorded by Conquest and other historians of the Gulag, murders of the guards and mass breakouts did indeed occur, resulting in brief periods when the *zeks* set up an independent commune of their own.

As an artist, Solzhenitsyn is careful to portray his representative Shukhov as a simple man, not so dissimilar in some ways from Tolstoy's soldier captive Karataev in *War and Peace*. When the convict who was once a captain in the Soviet Navy asks him with some curiosity if he believes in God, he matter-of-factly replies that of course he does, for who else makes the thunder, and causes stars at night to fall out of the sky? Shukhov's simplicity as an ordinary uneducated Russian is not emphasized or exaggerated, but it separates him effectively from his author, and prevents any merely intellectualized discussion of the phenomena of camp life. Everything is taken for granted, as Shukhov takes it. A personal note would weaken this impact, as Dostoevsky, too, was well aware when he created the all but anonymous convict who is the leading figure in *The House of the Dead*. For these writers the note to be avoided above all was that of outraged individuality – 'I was the man, I suffered, I was there' – which in many accounts of similar horrors, particularly in Europe or America, can seem almost a species of self-advertisement. There is no trace of that in Solzhenitsyn's story, although in his later writings he does not, of course, attempt to avoid appearing in his own person and giving – indeed preaching – his own sermon on what must be done for Russia, and in order to save Russia.

The present edition of *One Day in the Life of Ivan Denisovich* represents the complete and canonical version of the story. In *Novy Mir* it appeared first in amended form, because the magazine's editorial board were still fearful of the reaction of the censorship, even though they had been granted from on high the go-ahead to print the story. Khrushchev himself bore a major part of the responsibility, under Stalin, for the liquidation of the *kulak* class of well-to-do peasants during the purges; and though he wished to undermine the status of his old boss, he did not want too many uncomfortable details to emerge which might reflect upon himself. And so *Novy Mir* suppressed the fact that Tyurin, the leader of Shukhov's work-gang, had been sent to the camps solely for being the son of a *kulak*.

In the same way the full version gives us the whole story of how Shukhov himself comes to be inside. As a common soldier in the Great Patriotic War he had been captured by the Germans, but escaped and rejoined the Red Army, where he was promptly accused of being a spy. Since he would not admit this voluntarily he was beaten until he was forced to sign a confession to save his life. In this complete text we learn also that Baptists were given an automatic twenty-five years for their faith alone; and that Senka's 'crime' consisted in having been liberated from Buchenwald by the Americans, and thus having been associated with foreigners.

One Day in the Life of Ivan Denisovich is a book that will last as long as Russian literature. And the Russians, in the course of their tormented history, have not only produced so many moving literary masterpieces, but in so doing have influenced literature and human consciousness throughout the world.

John Bayley

SELECT BIBLIOGRAPHY

There are several full-scale biographies of Solzhenitsyn. Michael Scammell's *Solzhenitsyn*, W. W. Norton, New York, 1984/Hutchinson, London, 1985, is a comprehensive study, recently succeeded by D. M. Thomas's *Alexander Solzhenitsyn*, St Martin's Press, New York, 1998/Little, Brown and Company, London, 1998, which contains information hitherto unavailable. Readers in search of a more intimate portrait may like to complement these substantial volumes with the slighter but fascinating memoir by Natalya Reshetovskaya, *Sanya: My Life with Alexander Solzhenitsyn*, tr. Elena Ivanoff, Bobbs-Merrill, Indianapolis, 1975/Hart-Davis, London, 1977.

Perhaps the best accounts of Solzhenitsyn's life are to be found in his own works which are frequently autobiographical in temper if not in detail, not least *One Day in the Life of Ivan Denisovich* itself. Other texts which throw light on the man are *The Oak and the Calf* and *The Red Wheel*.

For the larger perspective on life in the camps, the daunting three volumes of *The Gulag Archipelago* are indispensable if exhausting. An outsider's view supporting Solzhenitsyn's account with other testimony and chilling statistics is provided by Robert Conquest's magnificent and terrible book *The Great Terror*, Macmillan, London, 1968 (revised 1990), one of the first to provide incontrovertible detailed proof that the Gulag existed.

CHRONOLOGY

DATE	AUTHOR'S LIFE	LITERARY CONTEXT
1918	Alexander Isaiyevich Solzhenitsyn born in Kislovodsk in the Caucasus, the son of an army officer (11 December).	1918 Blok: 'The Twelve'.
		1919 Reed: *Ten Days that Shook the World.*
		1921 Zamyatin: *We.*
		Tsvetaeva: *Mileposts.*
		1922 Joyce: *Ulysses.*
		Mandelstam: *Tristia.*
		Hašek: *The Good Soldier Švejk.*
		Bely: *Petersburg.*
		Pasternak: *My Sister Life.*
		1923 Gorky: *My Universities.*
1924	Moves with his mother to Rostov-on-Don.	1924 Trotsky: *Literature and Revolution.*
		Mann: *The Magic Mountain.*
		Bulgakov: *The White Guard.*
		1925 Kafka: *The Trial.*
		1926 Kafka: *The Castle.*
		Babel: *Red Cavalry.*
		Tsvetaeva: *The Ratcatcher.*
		1928 Ilf and Petrov: *Twelve Chairs.*
		1929 Hemingway: *A Farewell to Arms.*
		Remarque: *All Quiet on the Western Front.*
		Sholokov: *And Quiet Flows the Don.*
		Mayakovsky: *The Bedbug.*
		1930 Nabokov: *The Spy.*
		Mayakovsky: *The Bathhouse.*
		Suicide of Mayakovsky.
		Freud: *Civilization and its Discontents.*
		1931 Pasternak: *Safe Conduct.*
		Mandelstam: *Journey to Armenia.*

1917 February Revolution; abdication of Nicholas II; Lenin's return to Russia; October (Bolshevik) Revolution.

1918 Lenin transfers seat of government from St Petersburg to Moscow. Elected Constituent Assembly forcibly suppressed. Creation of Red Army. Peace of Brest-Litovsk between Russia and Germany (March). The Tsar and his family murdered by the Bolsheviks (July). Civil war between Reds and Whites (to 1921). World War I ends (November).

1919 Treaty of Versailles. Lenin's campaign of 'Red Terror'.

1920 League of Nations formed.

1921 Lenin launches NEP (New Economic Policy).

1922 Establishment of USSR. Stalin General Secretary of Communist Party Central Committee. Mussolini forms Fascist government in Italy.

1923 German financial crisis. Failure of Nazi Munich *putsch*.

1924 Death of Lenin.

1926 Trotsky expelled from Politburo. Germany admitted to League of Nations. General Strike in Britain.

1928 Stalin *de facto* dictator. First Five Year Plan in USSR.

1929 Wall Street Crash. Stalin's enforced collectivization of agriculture begins; millions lose their lives; liquidation of the *kulaks* (prosperous peasants).

1931 Trial of Mensheviks.

DATE	AUTHOR'S LIFE	LITERARY CONTEXT
		1932 Huxley: *Brave New World.* Céline: *Journey to the End of the Night.* Kataev: *Time Forward!* Tsvetaeva: *The Poet and Time; Art in the Light of Conscience.* 1933–4 Zoshchenko: 'Youth Restored; 'The Story of a Reforging'. 1935–40 Akhmatova: *Requiem.*
1936–41	Reads Mathematics and Physics at Rostov University. Begins correspondence course with Institute of Philosophy, Literature and History in Moscow. Marries Natalya Alekseyevna Reshetovskaya (1940), a fellow-student at Rostov.	1936 Bulgakov's *Molière* banned after only seven performances. 1937 Ivanov: *Sailing to the Island of Cytherea.* 1938 Nabokov: *Invitation to a Beheading.* Arrest and disappearance of Mandelstam. 1939 Arrest and disappearance of Babel. Joyce: *Finnegans Wake.* 1940 Hemingway: *For Whom the Bell Tolls.* Koestler: *Darkness at Noon.* Akhmatova: *From Six Books; Poem without a Hero* (to 1962).
1941	Conscripted as a private soldier (October).	1941 Suicide of Tsvetaeva.
1942–5	Graduates from Artillery School (1942). Serves continuously on the front, winning two decorations, and rising to rank of captain.	1942 Camus: *The Stranger.* 1943 Zoshchenko: *Before Sunrise.* 1944 Borges: *Fictions.*
1945	Arrested and sentenced to eight years in labour camp after making derogatory remarks about Stalin in a letter.	1945 Orwell: *Animal Farm.* Sartre: *The Age of Reason; The Reprieve.*
1946–50	Working as a mathematician in prison research institute.	
		1947 Camus: *The Plague.*

CHRONOLOGY

1932 Severe famine in the Ukraine (to 1934). Union of Soviet Writers founded. Proletarian writers' organizations banned. Election of Roosevelt in USA. Nazis become largest party in German Reichstag.

1933 USA recognizes Soviet government. Second Five Year Plan. Roosevelt announces 'New Deal'. Hitler becomes German Chancellor.

1934 Assassination of Kirov. First Congress of Union of Soviet Writers.

1935 Nuremberg Laws depriving Jews of citizenship and rights.

1936–8 Moscow show-trials of leading Party members; execution of Zinoviev and Kamenev. Large-scale liquidation of card-holding Communists in Stalin's 'Great Terror'. Hitler and Mussolini form Rome–Berlin Axis. Outbreak of Spanish Civil War (to 1939).

1937 Japanese invasion of China.

1938 Germany annexes Austria; Munich crisis. Trial and execution of Bukharin and others in USSR.

1939 Soviet–German Pact (August); Hitler's invasion of Poland; outbreak of World War II. Soviet invasion of Eastern Poland.
Soviet–Finn Winter War.

1940 Fall of France; Battle of Britain. Massacre of 15,000 Polish officers near Kalinin by order of Soviet government. Annexation of Baltic states. Trotsky assassinated in Mexico.

1941 Japanese attack Pearl Harbor; USA enters war. Hitler invades USSR. Fall of Kiev. Siege of Leningrad (to 1944).

1942 Rommel defeated at El Alamein. German army defeated at Stalingrad.

1943 Allied invasion of Italy.

1944 Allied landings in Normandy. Warsaw rising.

1945 Soviet troops take Berlin. Atomic bombs dropped on Hiroshima and Nagasaki. End of World War II.

1946 USSR extends influence over eastern Europe. Beginning of Cold War. Expansion of concentration camp system. Central Committee decree attacking Akhmatova and Zoshchenko.

1947 Indian independence.

1948 Jewish state of Israel comes into existence. Russian blockade of West Berlin. Yugoslavia under Tito expelled from Comintern. Apartheid introduced in South Africa.

ALEXANDER SOLZHENITSYN

DATE	AUTHOR'S LIFE	LITERARY CONTEXT
		1949 Orwell: *Nineteen Eighty-Four*. Greene: *The Third Man*.
1950–52	Transferred to camp in Kazakhstan. Works as a bricklayer and in a machine shop. Stomach cancer diagnosed and operated on.	1951 Salinger: *The Catcher in the Rye*. 1952 Beckett: *Waiting for Godot*.
1953–6	Release from labour camp followed by internal exile in Kazakhstan, where he teaches in local school.	1953 Bellow: *The Adventures of Augie March*. 1954 Amis: *Lucky Jim*. Grossman: *In a Just Cause*. 1955 Nabokov: *Lolita*. 1956 Dudintsev: *Not by Bread Alone*.
1957–9	Formally rehabilitated. Writes *One Day in the Life of Ivan Denisovich*. Teaches science in Ryazan.	1958 Pasternak: *Doctor Zhivago*. Lampedusa: *The Leopard*. Kerouac: *On the Road*. Achebe: *Things Fall Apart*. Bellow: *Henderson the Rain King*. 1959 Grass: *The Tin Drum*. 1960 Updike: *Rabbit, Run*. 1961 Heller: *Catch-22*. Naipaul: *A House for Mr Biswas*. Yevtushenko: 'Babi Yar'.
1962	*Ivan Denisovich* published in *Novy Mir*.	1962 Nabokov: *Pale Fire*. Yevtushenko: 'The Heirs of Stalin'.
1963	Publication of 'Matryona's Place' and 'An Incident at Krechetovka Station'. *Ivan Denisovich* published in the West.	1964 Bellow: *Herzog*. Dombrovsky: *The Keeper of Antiquities*. 1966 Nabokov: *Speak, Memory*. Bulgakov: *The Master and Margarita*.
1967	Denounces censorship in open letter to Fourth Congress of Writers' Union and demands that the Union protect its members.	1967 Márquez: *One Hundred Years of Solitude*. Ginzburg: *Journey into the Whirlwind*.

CHRONOLOGY

DATE	AUTHOR'S LIFE	LITERARY CONTEXT
1968	Publication in the West of *Cancer Ward* and *The First Circle*.	
1969	Expelled from the Soviet Writers' Union. Separates from Reshetovskaya and lives with Natalya Svetlova, a mathematician, by whom he later has three sons. His play, *The Love Girl and the Innocent*, published in the West.	1969 Nabokov: *Ada or Ardor: A Family Chronicle.* Trifonov: *The Exchange.*
1970	Awarded Nobel Prize for Literature but unable to attend the ceremony in Stockholm.	1970 N. Mandelstam: *Hope Against Hope.* Kuznetsov: *Babi Yar.*
1971	*August 1914* (first book of an epic novel, 'The Red Wheel') published in the West.	1971 Updike: *Rabbit Redux.* 1972 N. Mandelstam: *Hope Abandoned.* Platonov: *Chevengur.*
1973	KGB discover and confiscate a copy of *The Gulag Archipelago*, whereupon Solzhenitsyn authorizes its Western publication. *Candle in the Wind*, a play, also published.	1973 Pynchon: *Gravity's Rainbow.* Platonov: *The Foundation Pit.*
1974	Expelled from Soviet Union; lives in Zürich. Continues work on 'The Red Wheel'.	1975 Levi: *The Periodic Table.* Voynovich: *Ivan Chonkin* (to 1979).
1976	*Lenin in Zürich.* Settles in Vermont.	1976 Zinoviev: *Yawning Heights.* Rasputin: *Farewell to Matyora.* 1977 Morrison: *Song of Solomon.* 1978 Shalamov: *Kolyma Tales.* Trifonov: *The Old Man.* Tendryakov: *Death of the Boss.* Greene: *The Human Factor.* Bitov: *Pushkin House.* Dombrovsky: *Faculty of Superfluous Things.* 1979 Calvino: *If on a winter's night a traveler.*
1980	*The Oak and the Calf* (autobiography).	1980 Aksyonov: *The Burn.* Grossman: *Life and Fate.* 1981 Updike: *Rabbit Is Rich.* Rushdie: *Midnight's Children.* Aksyonov: *The Island of Crimea.*

CHRONOLOGY

1968 Student unrest in USA and throughout Europe. Soviet invasion of Czechoslovakia. Underground journal *The Chronicle of Current Events* established; birth of human rights movement in USSR.
1969 Americans land first man on the moon.

1971 Mass Jewish demonstration at Supreme Soviet; large-scale Jewish emigration to Israel begins.
1972 Strategic Arms Limitation Treaty (SALT) signed by US and USSR.

1975 End of Vietnam War. USSR and Western powers sign Helsinki Agreement.

1977 Charter 77 signed by 241 Czech intellectuals.

1979 Margaret Thatcher first woman Prime Minister in UK. Carter and Brezhnev sign SALT-2. Soviet occupation of Afghanistan.
1980 Solidarity union under Lech Walesa stages strikes in Gdansk, Poland.

DATE	AUTHOR'S LIFE	LITERARY CONTEXT
		1982 Levi: *If not Now, When?*
		1984 Kundera: *The Unbearable Lightness of Being.*
		1986 Brodsky: *Less Than One.*
		1987 Rybakov: *Children of the Arbat.*
		Dudintsev: *White Clothing.*
		1988 Rushdie: *The Satanic Verses.*
		Brodsky: *To Urania: Selected Poems.*
		Sharansky: *Fear No Evil.*
1989	*Novy Mir* publishes Solzhenitsyn's Nobel Lectures, followed by *The Gulag Archipelago.*	1989 Tolstaya: *On the Golden Porch.*
		Grossman: *Forever Flowing.*
1990	Citizenship restored. At the invitation of Komsomolskaya Pravda writes manifesto *Rebuilding Russia.* 'The Red Wheel' appears in the USSR (*August 1914, October 1916, March 1917*), plus Russian editions of *The First Circle* and *Cancer Ward.*	1990 Updike: *Rabbit at Rest.* Zinoviev: *Perestroika in Partygrad.* Sakharov: *Memoirs.* 1991 Tolstaya: *Sleepwalker in a Fog.* Berberova: *The Italics are Mine.*
1994	Returns to Russia for the first time since his exile.	

CHRONOLOGY

ONE DAY IN THE LIFE OF
IVAN DENISOVICH

THE HAMMER banged reveille on the rail outside camp HQ at five o'clock as always. Time to get up. The ragged noise was muffled by ice two fingers thick on the windows and soon died away. Too cold for the warder to go on hammering.

The jangling stopped. Outside it was still as dark as when Shukhov had got up in the night to use the bucket – pitch black, except for three yellow lights visible from the window, two in the perimeter, one inside the camp.

For some reason they were slow unlocking the hut, and he couldn't hear the usual sound of the orderlies mounting the slop tub on poles to carry it out.

Shukhov never overslept. He was always up at the call. That way he had an hour and a half all to himself before work parade – time for a man who knew his way around to earn a bit on the side. He could stitch covers for somebody's mittens from a piece of old lining. Take some rich foreman his felt boots while he was still in his bunk (save him hopping round barefoot, fishing them out of the heap after drying). Rush round the storerooms looking for odd jobs – sweeping up or running errands. Go to the mess to stack bowls and carry them to the washers-up. You'd get something to eat, but there were too many volunteers, swarms of them. And the worst of it was that if there was anything left in a bowl you couldn't help licking it. Shukhov never for a moment forgot what his

3

first foreman Kuzyomin had told him. An old camp-wolf, twelve years inside by 1943. One day round the camp-fire in a forest clearing he told the reinforcements fresh from the front: "It's the law of the *taiga* here lads. But a man *can* live here, just like anywhere else. Know who pegs out first? The guy who licks out bowls, puts his faith in the sickbay, or squeals to godfather.*"

He was stretching it a bit there, of course. A stoolie will always get by, whoever else bleeds for him.

Shukhov always got up at once. Not today though. Hadn't felt right since the night before – had the shivers, and some sort of ache. And hadn't got really warm all night. In his sleep he kept fancying he was seriously ill, then feeling a bit better. Kept hoping morning would never come.

But it arrived on time.

Some hope of getting warm with a thick scab of ice on the windows, and white cobwebs of hoar frost where the walls of the huge hut met the ceiling.

Shukhov still didn't get up. He lay up top on a four-man bunk, with his blanket and jacket over his head, and both feet squeezed into one turned-in sleeve of his jerkin. He couldn't see anything but he knew from the sounds just what was going on in the hut and in his own gang's corner. He heard the orderlies trudging heavily down the corridor with the tub that held eight pails of slops. Light work for the unfit, they call it, but just try getting the thing out without spilling it! And that bump means Gang 75's felt boots are back from the drying room. And here come ours – today's our turn to get our boots dried out. The foreman and his deputy pulled their boots on in silence except for the bunk creaking under them. Now the

*Political officer in charge of the informers' network

deputy would be off to the bread-cutting room, and the foreman to see the work-assigners at HQ.

He did that every day, but today was different, Shukhov remembered. A fateful day for Gang 104: would they, or wouldn't they be shunted from the workshops they'd been building to a new site, the so-called "Sotsgorodok"★. This Sotsgorodok was a bare field kneedeep in snow, and for a start you'd be digging holes, knocking in fence posts and stringing barbed wire round them to stop yourself running away. After that – get building.

You could count on a month with nowhere to go for a warm, not so much as a dog kennel. You wouldn't even be able to light a fire out in the open – where would the fuel come from? Your only hope would be to dig, dig, dig for all you were worth.

The foreman went off to try and fix it, looking anxious. Maybe he can get some gang less quick off the mark dumped out there? You could never do a deal emptyhanded, of course. Have to slip the senior work-assigner half a kilo of fatback. Maybe a kilo, even.

Might as well give it a try – wander over to the sickbay and wangle a day off. Every bone in my body is aching.

Ah, but who's duty-warder today?

Oh yes. It's Ivan-and-a-half, the thin, lanky sergeant with black eyes. First time you saw him you were terrified, but when you got to know him he was the easiest of the lot – never put you in the hole, never dragged you off to the disciplinary officer. So lie in a bit longer, till it's time for Hut 9 to go to the mess.

The bunk swayed and trembled. Two men getting up at once: Shukhov's neighbour up top, Alyoshka the Baptist, and ex-Captain (Second Rank) Buynovsky.

★Socialist Settlement

The orderlies, oldish men, had carried out both night buckets and were now wrangling over who should fetch the hot water. They bickered like shrewish women. The welder from Gang 20 slung a boot and barked at them: "If you two deadbeats don't shut up I'll do it for you."

The boot hit a post with a thud, and the old men fell silent.

The deputy foreman of the gang next to them gave a low growl: "Vasily Fyodorich! Those rats in the foodstore have really diddled us this time. It was four nine hundreds, now it's only three. Who's got to go short?"

He said it quietly, but the whole gang heard and held its breath. Somebody would find a slice missing that evening.

Shukhov just lay there, on the tight-packed sawdust in his mattress. Wish it would make up its mind: wish I could either get a raging fever, or these aches and pains would go away. This is neither one thing nor the other.

While the Baptist was still whispering his prayers Buynovsky came in from the latrine and joyfully brought the bad news to no one in particular.

"Hang in there, shipmates! It's a good thirty below!"

That did it. Shukhov made up his mind to go to the sickbay.

But at that very moment the hand of authority whipped his jerkin and his blanket away. Shukhov threw off the jacket that covered his face and raised himself on one elbow. Down below, with his head on the level of the upper bunk, stood the gaunt Tartar.

Must have come on duty out of turn and sneaked up quietly.

"Shcha – eight hundred and fifty-four," the Tartar read out from the white patch on the back of the black jacket. "Three days in the hole, normal working hours."

His unmistakable strangled voice could be heard all over the half-dark hut – not all of the lightbulbs were burning – where two hundred men slept on half a hundred bug-ridden bunks. All those who had not risen yet were suddenly in a tearing hurry to dress.

"What for, citizen warder?" Shukhov asked, with more self-pity in his voice than he really felt.

Normal working hours was only half-punishment. You got warm food, and there was no time for brooding. Full punishment was when you weren't taken out to work.

"Didn't get up at the signal, did you? Report to HQ fast." He gave his explanation in a lazy drawl because he and Shukhov and everybody else knew perfectly well what the punishment was for.

The Tartar's hairless, crumpled face was blank. He turned round to look for victims but whether they were in half-darkness or under a lightbulb, on lower or upper bed shelves, all of them were stuffing their legs into black padded trousers with number patches on the left knee, or, already dressed, buttoning themselves up and hurrying towards the door to wait for the Tartar outside.

If Shukhov had done something to deserve it he wouldn't have minded so much. What upset him was that he was always one of the first up. But it was no good asking the Tartar to let him off, he knew that. He went on begging, for form's sake, standing there in the padded trousers he'd kept on all night (they had a shabby, greasy patch of their own stitched on above the left knee, with the number Shcha-854 traced on it in faded black ink), put on his jerkin (it had two similar numbers on it – one on the chest, one on the back), picked his boots out of the pile on the floor, put on his hat (with another such numbered rag on the front) and followed the Tartar outside.

All the men in Gang 104 saw Shukhov being led out, but nobody said a word: what good would it do, whatever you said? The foreman might have put in a word for him, but he wasn't there. Shukhov himself said nothing to anybody – he didn't want to irritate the Tartar. His messmates would have the sense to save his breakfast.

They went out together.

The mist in the frosty air took your breath away. Two big searchlights from watchtowers in opposite corners crossed beams as they swept the compound. Lights were burning around the periphery, and inside the camp, dotted around in such numbers that they made the stars look dim.

The snow squeaked under the boots of the *zeks*** hurrying about their business – to the latrine, to the storeroom, to the parcel room, to hand in meal they wanted cooked separately. Heads were drawn well down into shoulders, jackets buttoned tight. Their owners were chilled not so much by the frost as by the thought that they would be outside all day in it.

The Tartar marched steadily on in his old greatcoat with grubby blue shoulder tabs. The frost didn't seem to trouble him.

They walked by the high board fence round the BUR (the camp's stone punishment cell), past the barbed-wire fence that protected the camp bakery from the prisoners, past the corner of the staff hut where a frosted length of rail dangled at the end of a thick wire, past the frost-covered thermometer hanging on another post, in a sheltered spot so that it would not fall too low. Shukhov squinted hopefully at the milk-white tube; if it showed forty-one below they weren't supposed to be marched out to work. But it was nowhere near forty today.

*zek – (prison camp slang) convict

They went into the HQ hut and straight through to the warders' room. It was just as Shukhov had guessed on the way. He wasn't bound for the hole – it was just that the floor of the warders' room needed washing. The Tartar announced that he forgave Shukhov and ordered him to clean it.

Washing the floor was a job for the hut orderly, a *zek* who wasn't sent out to work. But he had made himself so much at home in the HQ hut that he had access to the offices of the major, the disciplinary officer and the godfather, made himself useful to them, heard a few things even the warders did not know, so for some time now he'd regarded cleaning floors for mere warders as demeaning. They'd sent for him a time or two, then realised how things stood and started "pulling" one or another of the working prisoners to clean the floor.

The heat from the stove in the warders' room was fierce. Two warders, stripped down to their dirty tunics, were playing draughts, and a third, still wearing his tightly belted sheepskin coat and felt boots, was asleep on a narrow bench.

Shukhov happily thanked the Tartar for forgiving him. "Thank you, citizen warder! I'll never sleep in again."

The rule was simple: leave as soon as you finish. Now that Shukhov had a job to do his body seemed to have stopped aching. He took the bucket, and just as he was, without mittens, (he'd left them under the pillow in the rush) went out to the well.

Several of the foremen reporting to the PPS* had crowded round the post, and one, a youngish man, ex-Hero of the Soviet Union, had shinned up it and was rubbing the frost off the thermometer.

*Production Planning Section

Advice reached him from down below.

"Don't breathe on it, man, or it'll go up."

"Go up? In a pig's ear. That doesn't make any difference."

Shukhov's foreman, Tyurin, was not among them. He put his bucket down, worked his hands into opposite sleeves, and watched curiously.

The man up the pole said hoarsely: "Twenty-seven and a half, the bastard."

He looked harder to make sure, and jumped down.

"Bullshit. It doesn't work properly," somebody said. "Think they'd hang it where we can see it if it did?"

The foremen went their ways and Shukhov trotted to the well. His earflaps were down but not tied under his chin and the frost made his ears ache.

There was such thick ice round the well-head that the bucket would hardly go into the hole. The rope was as stiff as a pole.

When he got back to the warders' quarters with his streaming bucket there was no feeling in his hands. He plunged them into the well-water and felt a little warmer.

The Tartar was missing, but four others had gathered. Draughts and sleep had been forgotten, and they were discussing how much wheat they would be given in January. (There was a shortage of foodstuffs in the settlement, but the warders were able to buy extra supplies at discount prices, although they had long ago used up their ration coupons.)

One of them broke off to yell at Shukhov.

"Pull the door to, you shit! There's a draught here!"

Wouldn't be a good idea at all to start the day with his boots wet, and he had no others to change into, even if he could dash over to the hut. Shukhov had seen all sorts of arrangements about footwear during his eight years inside: you might walk round all winter without felt boots, you might never even see a pair of ordinary shoes, just birch-bark clogs or the Chelyabinsk Tractor Factory type – strips off old tyres that left tread marks in the snow. But this time round things had worked out pretty well. Last October he'd tagged along to the clothing store with the deputy foreman and got hold of a pair of stout shoes with hard toecaps and room for two warm footrags in each. He'd walked around for a whole week as though it was his birthday, making a clatter with his new heels. Then in December felt boots had turned up as well: life was a bed of roses, no need to die just yet. So some fiend in the accounts office had whispered in the big man's ear: let them have the boots, but only if they hand their shoes in: it's against the rules for a *zek* to have two pairs at once. So Shukhov had faced a choice: either wear shoes all winter, or turn them in and wear felt boots even when it thawed. He'd taken such good care of his nice new shoes, he'd greased them to make them soft ... he'd never missed anything so much in all those eight years. The shoes were all tossed on one big pile – no hope of getting your own pair back when spring came. It was just like the time when they rounded everybody's horses up for the *kolkhoz*.

Shukhov knew what to do this time: he stepped nimbly out of his felt boots, stood them in a corner, tossed his footrags after them, (his spoon tinkled as it hit the floor – he'd had to get ready for the hole in a hurry but he still hadn't forgotten his spoon) – and, barefoot, dived at the warders' feltbooted feet, generously splashing the floor around them with water from his floorcloth.

"Hey! Steady on, you crud," one of them said, drawing his feet up onto his chair.

"Rice, you say? The rice allowance is different. There's no comparison with wheat."

"Why are you using all that water, you idiot? What a way to wash a floor!"

"Never get it clean any other way, citizen warder. The dirt's eaten into the floor."

"Did you never see your old woman clean a floor, you filthy pig?"

Shukhov straightened up, holding the dripping floorcloth. He smiled innocently, showing the gaps left in his teeth by an attack of scurvy when he was on his last legs at Ust-Izhma in '43. He'd thought he was done for – a bleeding diarrhoea had drained all the strength out of him and he couldn't keep anything in his stomach. Now he only had a slight lisp to remind him of it all.

"They parted my old woman and me in '41, citizen officer. I don't even remember what she looks like."

"That's what this lot call cleaning a floor. The bastards can't do any damned thing properly, and they don't want to learn. They aren't worth the bread we give them. Feed them on shit, I would."

"Why the hell does it have to be washed every day, anyway? It never has time to get dry. Listen here, eight fifty-four! Just give it a once-over, don't make it too wet, and get the hell out of here!"

"Rice, man! There's no way you can compare it with wheat!"

Shukhov made a quick job of it.

There are two ends to a stick, and there's more than one way of working. If it's for human beings – make sure and do it properly. If it's for the big man – just make it look good.

Any other way we'd all have turned our toes up long ago, that's for sure.

Shukhov wiped the floorboards, leaving no dry patches, and without stopping to wring it out tossed the rag behind the stove. He pulled his boots on in the doorway, splashed the water out on the path along which the screws walked, and took a short cut past the bath house, past the dark, chilly recreation centre towards the mess hut.

He had to get to the sickbay while there was still time – he was aching all over again. And he mustn't let the warders catch him outside the mess hut: the camp commandant had given strict orders to pick up stragglers and shove them in the hole.

Funny thing – no big crowd, no queue, outside the mess today. Walk right in.

It was like a bath house inside – whenever the door opened, frosty air mingled with the steam from the skilly. Some work gangs were sitting at tables, others were blocking the aisles waiting for vacant places. Two or three workers from every gang shouted and shoved their way through the mob, carrying bowls of skilly and gruel on wooden trays and looking for a space to put them down on. Must be deaf, the blockhead, take that for jogging the tray and making me spill the stuff! That's it – use your free hand – give him one in the neck. That's the stuff! You there, don't get in the way looking for leftovers.

There's a young lad at that table over there crossing himself before he dips his spoon in. One of Bendera's* lot, must be. And a new boy at that. The older ones give it up when they've been inside a bit.

The Russians don't even remember which hand you cross yourself with.

It's cold sitting in the mess hut. Most men eat with their caps on, but they take their time, angling for gluey scraps

*Member of the Ukrainian nationalist underground

of rotten little fish under the leaves of frost-blackened cabbage, and spitting the bones onto the table. When there's a mountain of them somebody will sweep them off before the next gang sits down, and they will be crunched to powder underfoot.

Spitting bones out on the floor is considered bad manners.

There were pillars or stanchions down the middle of the hut (two rows of them). Fetyukov, a workmate of Shukhov's, sat by one looking after his breakfast for him. Fetyukov was one of the lowliest members of the gang – even Shukhov was a cut above him. Outwardly the gang all looked the same, all wearing identical black jackets with identical number patches, but underneath there were big differences. You'd never get Buynovsky to sit watching a bowl, and there were jobs that Shukhov left to those beneath him.

Fetyukov caught sight of him and gave up his seat with a sigh. "It's all gone cold. I nearly ate it for you, I thought you were in the hole."

He didn't wait around. He knew Shukhov would polish both bowls till they shone and leave nothing for him.

Shukhov drew his spoon from his boot. That spoon was precious, it had travelled all over the north with him. He'd cast it himself from aluminium wire in a sand mould and scratched on it "Ust-Izhma, 1944".

Next, he removed his cap from his shaven head – however cold it was he wouldn't let himself eat with his cap on – and stirred up his skilly, quickly checking what had found its way into his bowl. Could have been worse. Not ladled from the top of the cauldron, but not the dregs either. Fetyukov could have fished out the potato while he was guarding the bowl – be just like him!

The best you can ever say for skilly is that it's hot, but this time Shukhov's was cold. He started eating slowly, savouring it, just the same. If the roof burst into flames he still wouldn't hurry. Apart from sleep an old lag can call his life his own only for ten minutes at breakfast-time, five at lunch-time, and five more at supper-time.

The skilly didn't change from day to day. What was in it depended on which vegetable was stockpiled for winter. Last year they'd laid in nothing but carrots in brine – so from September to June it was carrots all the way. This time round it was black cabbage. June is when the *zek* eats best: the vegetables run out, and there's meal instead. The leanest time is July, when chopped nettles go into the pot.

There was nothing much left of the little fish, only bones: the flesh had come away and dissolved, except for scraps of head and tail. Shukhov left neither flesh nor scales on the brittle skeletons. He champed and sucked them between his lips, then spat them out on the table. He ate every bit of every fish, gills, tails, even eyes if they were where they should be, but if they had boiled out of the head and were floating loose in the bowl – the big, fish-eyes goggling at him – he wouldn't eat them. The others laughed at him for it.

He'd been thrifty today. He hadn't gone to the hut for his ration and was eating without bread. He could scoff it by itself later on. More filling that way.

The second course was magara gruel. It had congealed into a solid bar. Shukhov broke bits off. Magara is bad enough hot – tastes of nothing, leaves you feeling empty. Yellowish like wheat, but just grass really. Somebody's bright idea, serving it instead of meal. Seemed they got it from the Chinese. Maybe three hundred grammes, boiled weight. So make the best of it: call it what you like, it was all you were getting.

Shukhov licked his spoon clean and returned it to his boot, then put on his cap and made for the sickbay.

The camp lights had chased the stars from the sky, and it was as dark as before. The broad beams from the corner towers were still quartering the compound. When they first set up this "special"* camp, the guards still had stacks of army surplus flares, and as soon as the light faded they would fill the air over the camp with white, green and red fires. It was like a battlefield. Then they stopped throwing the things around. Probably cost too much.

It was just as dark as at reveille, but an experienced eye could tell from all sorts of little signs that the signal for work parade would soon be sounded. Limpy's assistant (Limpy, the mess orderly, was able to keep and feed a helper) went to call Hut 6 — those too unfit to leave the compound — to breakfast. The old artist with the little beard ambled off to the Culture and Education Department for brush and ink to paint numbers. Yet again the Tartar strode rapidly across the midway towards the staff hut. People were suddenly thinner on the ground — they were all skulking inside, warming themselves in the few sweet minutes left.

Shukhov dived into hiding round the corner of a hut: if the Tartar spotted him he'd give him hell again. You had to be wide awake all the time. Make sure a warder never saw you on your own, only as one of a crowd. He might be looking for somebody to do a job, or he might just want to take his spite out on you. They'd gone round every hut reading out the order: prisoners must doff their caps when they see a warder five paces away, and keep them off till they are two paces past him. Some warders wandered by blindly, but others made a meal of it. The

*Hard-labour camps for prisoners specifically charged with political crimes

hellhounds had hauled any number off to the cooler because of the "caps off" order. Better wait round the corner for a while.

The Tartar went past, and Shukhov had made up his mind to go to the sickbay when it suddenly dawned on him that he had arranged with the lanky Latvian in Hut 7 to buy two tumblers full of home-grown tobacco that morning. With so much to do it had gone clean out of his mind. The lanky Latvian had been given his parcel the night before, and by tomorrow there might be no tobacco left. It would be a month before he got another, and it was good stuff, just strong enough and sweet-smelling. A sort of reddish brown, it was.

Vexed with himself, Shukhov almost turned on his heel and went back to Hut 7. But the sickbay was quite close and he made for its porch at a trot.

The snow squeaked under his feet.

It was always so clean in the sickbay that you were afraid to tread on the floor. The walls were bright with white enamel paint, and all the fittings were white.

But the doctors' doors were all shut. Not out of bed yet, you could bet. The medical orderly on duty, a young fellow called Kolya Vdovushkin, was sitting in a crisp white gown at a clean desk, writing. There was nobody else around.

Shukhov took off his cap as though to a superior officer. He had the old lag's habit of letting his eyes wander where they shouldn't, and he noticed that Kolya was writing lines of exactly the same length, leaving a margin and starting each one with a capital letter exactly below the beginning of the last. He knew right off, of course, that this wasn't work but something on the side. None of his business, though.

"It's like this, Nikolai Semyonich, I feel sort of poorly."

Shukhov looked embarrassed, as though he was on the scrounge.

Vdovushkin raised large mild eyes from his work. He was wearing a white cap, and a white overall with no number patches.

"Why so late? Why didn't you come last night? Don't you know there's no clinic in the morning? The sick list has gone over to PPS already."

Shukhov knew all that. He also knew that it was no easier to get off work in the evening.

"Yes, but Kolya, it didn't start hurting last night, when it ought to have."

"What didn't? Where's the pain?"

"Well, when I try to put my finger on it I can't say where it is. I just feel poorly all over."

Shukhov wasn't one of those who haunted the sickbay and Vdovushkin knew it. But he was authorised to let off only two men in the morning. And there were already two names under the greenish glass on top of the desk. With a line drawn under them.

"Well, you should have started worrying about it earlier. What's the good of coming right before work parade? Here!"

A number of thermometers had been inserted into a jar through a slit in its gauze cover. Vdovushkin drew one of them out, wiped off the solution, and gave it to Shukhov.

Shukhov sat on the very edge of a bench by the wall, just far enough not to tip over with it. He had chosen this uncomfortable place unconsciously, intending to show that he wasn't at home in the sickbay and would make no great demands on it.

Vdovushkin went on writing.

The sickbay was in the most out-of-the-way corner of the camp, and no sound whatsoever reached it: there was not even the ticking of a clock – prisoners are not allowed clocks. The big boys tell the time for them. You couldn't even hear mice scratching – they'd all been caught by the hospital cat, as was his duty.

Shukhov felt strange sitting under a bright light doing nothing for five whole minutes in such deep silence in such a clean room. He inspected the walls and found nothing there. He inspected his jerkin – the number on his breast had been almost rubbed away, he'd have to get it touched up before they pounced on him. With his free hand he felt his face – his beard had come on fast in the last ten days. So what, it wasn't in his way. It would be bath day again in three days' time and he'd get a shave then. Why waste time waiting your turn at the barber's? He had nobody to make himself pretty for.

Looking at Vdovushkin's snow-white cap Shukhov remembered the field hospital on the River Lovat – he'd gone there with a damaged jaw, and gone back into the line of his own free will, stupid clod, when he could have had five days' rest.

His one dream now was to fall sick for two or three weeks. Not fatally, of course, and he didn't want an operation. Just sick enough to be put in the hospital. He could see himself lying there for three weeks without stirring, being fed on clear beef broth. Suit him nicely, that would.

Only now, he remembered, there was no lying up even in hospital. A new doctor, Stepan Grigorich, had arrived with one of the recent batches. He was fast and furious, always on the boil himself, and he made sure the patients got no peace. One of his bright ideas was turning out the patients who could walk to work in the hospital precincts – putting up fences, laying paths, shovelling extra soil onto flowerbeds, and – in the winter – banking snow to keep the ground warm. Work, he reckoned, was the best medicine of the lot.

Work is what horses die of. Everybody should know that. If he ever had to bust a gut bricklaying he'd soon quieten down.

Meanwhile Vdovushkin went on with his writing. It was in fact "something on the side", but nothing that Shukhov would have comprehended. He was copying out his long new poem. He had put the finishing touches to it the night before and had promised to show it to the new doctor, Stepan Grigorich, that morning.

It was the sort of thing that happens only in camp: Stepan Grigorich had advised Vdovushkin to call himself a medical orderly and had given him the job. Vdovushkin was now practising intravenous injections on ignorant prisoners and meek Lithuanians and Estonians, to whom it would never occur that a medical orderly could be nothing of the kind, but a former student of literature, arrested in his second year of university. Stepan Grigorich wanted him to write in prison what he hadn't had a chance to write outside.

The signal for work parade could barely be heard through double windows shuttered by white ice, but Shukhov sighed and stood up. He still felt shivery, but he could see that he wasn't going to get away with it. Vdovushkin reached for the thermometer and looked at it.

"There you are – neither one thing nor the other. Thirty-seven point two. If it was thirty-eight nobody would argue. I can't let you off, but you can stay if you feel like risking it. The doctor will look you over and let you off if he thinks you're ill, but if he reckons you're fit, you'll be in the hole for malingering. I'd go to work if I were you."

Shukhov rammed on his hat and left without a word or a nod.

Can a man who's warm understand one who's freezing?

The frost was cruel. A stinging haze wrapped around him and set him coughing. The air temperature was twenty-seven below and Shukhov's temperature was thirty-seven above. No holds barred!

He trotted to the hut. The midway was empty right across. The whole camp looked empty. It was that last, short, painfully sweet moment when there was no escape but everybody still pretended that work parade would never come. The guards would still be sitting in their warm barracks, resting their sleepy heads on their rifle butts. Teetering on watchtowers in such a hard frost was no fun either. The sentries in the main guard house would be shovelling more coal into the stove. The warders would be smoking one last cigarette before the body search. And the *zeks*, dressed up in all their rags and tatters, girded with lengths of rope, muffled from chin to eyes in facerags to keep the frost out, would be lying, boots and all, on top of their blankets, eyes shut, lost to the world. Waiting for the foreman to yell "We're off!"

Gang 104 dozed with the rest of Hut 9. Except for Pavlo, the deputy foreman, who sat moving his lips as he totted something up with a pencil, and Alyoshka the well-washed Baptist, Shukhov's neighbour, who was reading the notebook into which he had copied half the New Testament.

Shukhov dashed in but without too much noise and went over to the deputy foreman's bed.

Pavlo raised his head.

"Didn't land in the hole, then, Ivan Denisovich? Still among the living?" (Western Ukrainians never learn. Even in the camps they speak to people politely.)

He picked up Shukhov's portion of bread from the
table and held it out. A little hillock of sugar had been
scooped onto it.

Shukhov was in a great hurry, but still thanked him
properly. (The deputy foreman was one of his bosses, and
more important to Shukhov than the camp commandant.) Nor was he in too much of a hurry to dip his lips in
the sugar and lick them, as he hoisted himself up with one
foot on the bed bracket to straighten his bedding, or to
view his bread ration from all angles and weigh it on his
hand in mid-air, wondering whether it contained the
regulation five hundred and fifty grammes. Shukhov had
drawn a few thousand bread rations in jails and prison
camps, and though he'd never had the chance to weigh his
portion on the scales, and anyway was too timid to kick
up a fuss and demand his rights, he knew better than most
prisoners that a bread-cutter who gave full measure
wouldn't last long at the job. Every portion was under-
weight – the only question was by how much. Twice a
day you looked at it and tried to set your mind at rest.
Maybe they haven't robbed me blind this time? Maybe it's
only a couple of grammes short?

About twenty grammes light, Shukhov decided, and
broke the bread in two. He shoved one half into a little
white pocket stitched inside his jerkin (prison jerkins come
from the factory without pockets). The other half, saved
from breakfast, he thought of eating there and then, but
food swallowed in a hurry is food wasted, you feel no
fuller and it does nothing for you. He made as if to stow
the half-ration in his locker, but changed his mind when
he remembered that the hut orderlies had been beaten up
twice for stealing. A big hut is about as safe as an open
yard.

So without letting go of the bread Ivan Denisovich

slipped out of his boots, deftly leaving spoon and footrags in place, scrambled barefoot onto the top bunk, widened the hole in his mattress and hid his half-ration among the sawdust. Then he tugged off his cap and unsheathed a threaded needle – also well hidden. (They'd feel your cap during the body search. A warder had once pricked himself and nearly smashed Shukhov's skull in his rage.) Stitch, stitch, stitch and he'd tacked up the hole over the hidden half-ration. By then the sugar had melted in his mouth. Every fibre in his body was tensed to the utmost: the work-assigner would be bellowing at the door any moment now. His fingers were wonderfully nimble, and his mind raced ahead, planning his next moves.

The Baptist was reading his Bible, not altogether silently, but sort of sighing out the words. This was meant perhaps for Shukhov. (A bit like political agitators, these Baptists. Loved spreading the word.)

"But let none of you suffer as a murderer, or a thief, or a wrongdoer, or a mischief-maker: yet if one suffers as a Christian, let him not be ashamed, but under that name let him glorify God."*

Alyoshka was a champion at one thing: wiggling that little book of his into a crack in the wall so neatly that it had never been found by searching warders.

With the same rapid movements Shukhov draped his overcoat over the end of his bed, teased his mittens out from under the mattress, together with another pair of flimsy footrags, a rope and a rag with two tapes attached to it. He did a lovely job of smoothing down the bumps in the mattress (the sawdust was heavy and close-packed), tucked the blanket under all round, tossed the pillow into place, and, still barefoot, lowered himself and began

* 1 Peter 4

putting on his boots – first, though, the good, new footrags, with the worn ones over them.

That was when the foreman stood up and barked: "Rise and shine, one-o-four! Let's have you outside!"

Every man in the gang, nodding or not, rose to his feet, yawned and made for the door. After nineteen years inside, the foreman wouldn't hustle his men out a minute before time. When he said "out" you knew there was nothing else for it.

While his mates tramped wordlessly one after another into the corridor, then through the entryway out onto the porch, and the foreman of No. 20, taking his cue from Tyurin, called "all out" in turn, Shukhov had managed to pull his boots over the two layers of footrags, put his overcoat on over his jerkin, and tie a length of rope tightly round his waist. (If you arrived in a Special Camp with a leather belt it was taken away from you – not allowed.)

So he was ready on time, and caught up with the last of his gang as their numbered backs were passing through the door onto the porch. In single file, making no effort to keep up with each other, every man a fatty because he was muffled up in every garment he possessed, they trudged across to the midway with not a sound except for the crunch of snow underfoot.

It was still dark, although a greenish light was brightening in the east. A thin, treacherous breeze was creeping in from the same direction.

There is no worse moment than when you turn out for work parade in the morning. In the dark, in the freezing cold, with a hungry belly, and the whole day ahead of you. You lose the power of speech. You haven't the slightest desire to talk to each other.

The junior work-assigner was restlessly pacing the midway.

"Come on Tyurin, how long have we got to wait for you? Another go-slow, is it?"

Somebody like Shukhov might be afraid of the junior work-assigner, but Tyurin wasn't. Wouldn't waste breath on him in that frost. Just tramped ahead without a word. And the whole gang tramped after him: stamp, stamp, crunch, crunch.

Tyurin must have handed over the kilo of fatback, though – because looking at the other teams, you could see that 104 was in its old position. Some other lot, poorer and more stupid, would be shunted off to Sotsgorodok. It would be murder out there – twenty-seven below, with a mean wind blowing, no shelter, and no hope of a warm!

The foreman needed plenty of fatback – for the PPS, and to keep his own belly purring. He might not get parcels himself but he never went short. Every man in the gang who did get a parcel gave him a present right away.

It was that or perish.

The senior work-assigner was ticking off names on his board.

"One sick, Tyurin, twenty-three on parade?"

The foreman nodded. "Twenty-three."

Who was missing? Panteleyev. Who said he was sick, though?

A whisper went round the gang. Panteleyev, that son of a bitch, had stayed behind in camp again. He wasn't sick at all, the security officer had kept him back. He'd be squealing on somebody again.

Nothing to stop them sending for him later in the day and keeping him for three hours if necessary. Nobody would be there to see or hear. They could pretend he was in the sickbay.

The whole midway was black with prison jackets as the gangs slowly jostled each other towards the checkpoint.

Shukhov remembered that he'd meant to freshen up the
number on his jerkin, and squeezed through the crowd to
the other side of the road. Two or three *zeks* were queuing
up for the artist already. Shukhov stood behind them.
Those numbers were the plague of a *zek's* life. A warder
could spot him a long way off. One of the guards might
make a note of it. And if you didn't get it touched up in
time you were in the hole for not looking after it!

There were three artists in the camp. They painted
pictures for the bosses, free, and also took turns painting
numbers on work parade. This time it was the old man
with the little grey beard. The way his brush moved as he
painted a number on a cap made you think of a priest
anointing a man's forehead with holy oil. He would paint
for a bit and then stop to breathe into his glove. It was a
thin knitted glove, and his hand would get too numb to
trace the figures.

The artist renewed the "Shcha-854" on Shukhov's
jerkin. He wasn't far from the searchpoint, so he didn't
bother to fasten his jacket but overtook the rest of the
gang with his rope belt in his hand. He suddenly spotted a
chance of scrounging a butt: one of the gang, Tsezar, was
smoking a cigarette instead of his usual pipe. Shukhov
didn't ask straight out, though. Just took his stand near
Tsezar, half facing him and looking past him.

He was gazing at something in the distance, trying to
look uninterested, but seeing the cigarette grow shorter
and the red tip creep closer to the holder every time Tsezar
took an absent-minded drag.

That scavenger Fetyukov was there too, leeching onto
Tsezar, standing right in front of him and staring hot-eyed
at his mouth.

Shukhov had not a shred of tobacco left, and couldn't

see himself getting hold of any before evening. He was on tenterhooks. Right then he seemed to yearn for that dog-end more than for freedom itself, but he wouldn't lower himself like Fetyukov, wouldn't look at Tsezar's mouth.

Tsezar was a mixture of all nationalities. No knowing whether he was Greek, Jew or gypsy. He was still young. Used to make films, but they'd put him inside before he finished his first picture. He had a heavy black walrus moustache. They'd have shaved it off only he was wearing it when they photographed him for the record.

Fetyukov couldn't stand it any longer. "Tsezar Marko-vich," he drooled. "Save me just one little drag."

His face was twitching with greed.

Tsezar raised his half-closed eyelids and turned his dark eyes on Fetyukov. He'd taken to smoking a pipe to avoid this sort of thing – people barging in begging for the last drag. He didn't grudge them the tobacco, but he didn't like being interrupted when he was thinking. He smoked to set his mind racing in pursuit of some idea. But the moment he lit a cigarette he saw "leave a puff for me!" in several pairs of eyes.

He turned to Shukhov and said, "Here you are, Ivan Denisovich."

His thumb eased the glowing butt out of the short amber holder.

That was all Shukhov had been waiting for. He sprang into action and gratefully caught hold of the butt, keeping the other hand underneath for safety. He wasn't offended that Tsezar was too fussy to let him finish the cigarette in the holder. Some mouths are clean, others are dirty, and anyway his horny fingers could hold the glowing tip without getting burnt. The great thing was that he'd cut the scavenger Fetyukov out and was now inhaling smoke, with the hot ash beginning to burn his lips. Ah, lovely. The smoke seemed to reach every part of his hungry body, he felt it in his feet as well as in his head.

But no sooner had this blissful feeling pervaded his body than Ivan Denisovich heard a rumble of protest:

"They're taking our undershirts off us."

A *zek's* life was always the same. Shukhov was used to it: relax for a minute and somebody was at your throat.

What was this about undershirts? The camp commandant had issued them himself. No, it couldn't be right.

There were only two gangs ahead waiting to be searched, so everybody in 104 got a good view: the disciplinary officer, Lieutenant Volkovoy, walked over from HQ hut and barked at the warders. They had been frisking the men half-heartedly before Volkovoy appeared, but now they went mad, setting upon the prisoners like wild beasts, with the head warder yelling "Unbutton your shirts!"

Volkovoy was dreaded not just by the *zeks* and the warders but, so it was said, by the camp commandant himself. God had marked the scoundrel with a name to suit his wolfish looks. He was lanky, dark, beetle-browed, quick on his feet: he would pop up when you least expected him, shouting "Why are you all hanging around here?" There was no hiding from him. At one time he'd carried a lash, a plaited leather thing as long as your forearm. They said he thrashed people with it in the camp jail. Or else when *zeks* were huddled outside the door during the evening hut search he would creep up and slash you across the neck with it: "Why aren't you lined up properly, you scum?" The crowd would reel back like an ebbing wave. The whipped man would clutch his burning neck, wipe the blood away, and say nothing: he didn't want a spell in the hole as well.

Just lately he'd stopped carrying his lash for some reason.

In frosty weather body searches were usually less strict in the morning than in the evening; the prisoner simply undid his jacket and held its skirts away from his body. Prisoners advanced five at a time, and five warders stood ready for them. They slapped the sides of each *zek's* belted jerkin, and tapped the one permitted pocket on his right knee. They would be wearing gloves themselves, and if they felt something strange they didn't immediately pull it out but lazily asked what it was.

What would you expect to find on a *zek* in the morning? A knife? They don't carry knives out, they bring them in. Just make sure he hasn't got three kilogrammes of food on him, to run away with – that's all that matters in the morning. At one time they got so worried about the two hundred grammes every *zek* took with him for dinner that each gang was ordered to make a wooden chest to hold the lot. Why the bastards thought that would do any good was a mystery. They were probably just out to make life more miserable, give the men something extra to worry about. You took a bite and looked hard at your bread before you put it in the chest. But the pieces were still all alike, still just bread, so you couldn't help fretting all the way to work in case somebody switched rations. Men argued with each other and sometimes came to blows. Then one day three men helped themselves to a chest full of bread and escaped from a work site in a truck. The brass came to their senses, had the chests chopped up in the guard house, and let everybody carry his own ration again.

Another thing the searchers looked for in the morning: men wearing civilian dress under prison clothes. Never mind that everybody had been stripped of his civilian belongings long ago, and told that he'd get them back the day his sentence ended (a day nobody in that camp had yet seen).

And one other thing – prisoners carrying letters for free workers to smuggle out. Only if you searched everybody for letters you'd be messing about till dinner-time.

But Volkovoy only had to bawl out an order and the warders peeled off their gloves, made the prisoners unbelt the jerkins under which they were all hugging the warmth of the hut and unbutton their shirts, and set about feeling for anything hidden underneath contrary to regulations. A *zek* was allowed two shirts – shirt and undershirt – everything else must come off. That was the order from Volkovoy relayed from rank to rank. The teams that had gone past earlier were the lucky ones. Some of them were already through the gates, but for those left behind it was "Open up!" All those with too much on underneath must take it off right there in the cold.

They made a start, but the result was confusion: the gates had already been cleared and the guards were bawling "Hurry it up! Let's go!" So Volkovoy swallowed his wrath and let 104 off lightly: note down those wearing anything extra, and make them turn it in to the clothes store this evening together with an explanation in writing where and why they hid it.

Shukhov was wearing only camp issue anyway: go ahead, he told them silently, have a feel, nothing here, only a bare chest with a soul inside it. But a note was made of Tsezar's flannelette vest, and Buynovsky – surprise – had a little waistcoat or cummerbund of some sort. Buynovsky shouted at the top of his voice – he'd been used to torpedo-boats, and had spent less than three months in the camp.

"You have no right to make people undress in freezing cold! You don't know Article 9 of the Criminal Code!"

But they did have. They did know. It's you, brother, who don't know anything yet!

The captain kept blazing away at them: "You aren't real Soviet people!"

Volkovoy didn't mind Article 9, but at this he looked as black as a thundercloud.

"Ten days strict regime!" he shouted. "With effect from this evening," he told the head warder, lowering his voice.

They never like putting a man in the hole first thing in the morning: it means a loss of one man-shift. Let him sweat and strain all day, and sling him in the hole at night.

The jail house stood nearby, to the left of the midway: a stone building, with two wings. The second wing had been added that autumn – there wasn't room enough in just one. It was an eighteen-cell jail and there were walled-off recesses for solitary confinement. The rest of the camp was wood-built, only the jail was of stone.

Now that the cold had been let in under their shirts there was no getting rid of it. They had all muffled themselves up for nothing. And the dull pain in Shukhov's back would not let go. If only he could lie down there and then on a cot in the sickbay and sleep. He had no other wish in the world. Just a good heavy blanket.

The *zeks* stood near the gate buttoning and belting themselves with the guards outside yelling "Hurry it up! Let's go!"

And the work-assigner was also shoving them from behind and shouting "Let's go! Look alive!"

Through the first gate. Into the outer guarded area.

Through the second gate. Between the railings by the guard house.

"Halt!" roared the sentry. "Like a flock of sheep! Sort yourselves out in fives!"

By now the darkness was lifting. The convoy's bonfire was burning out. They always got a good fire going before work parade – so they could keep warm and see better to count.

One of the sentries counted them off in a loud, harsh voice: "First five! Second! Third!"

And the groups of five peeled off and moved forward in separate ranks so that, looking from the front or from behind, you saw five heads, five trunks and ten legs.

A second sentry stood by the railings opposite, silently checking the count.

A lieutenant also stood watching.

All this on behalf of the administration.

Every man was more precious than gold. A single head short behind the wire and your own head would make up for it.

The gang closed up again.

Now the escort party's sergeant was counting.

And again the groups of five detached themselves and went forward in separate ranks.

The assistant guard commander checked the count from the other side.

And a lieutenant double-checked.

All this on behalf of the convoy.

On no account must they make a mistake. Sign for one head too many and your own would make up the number.

There were escort troops all over the place. They held the Power-Station column in a semi-circular embrace, automatic weapons levelled, stuck right in your mug.

Then there were the handlers with their grey dogs. One dog bared its teeth as though laughing at the *zeks*. The convoy were all wearing short fur coats except for half a dozen in sheepskins. The whole shift shared the sheepskins – you put one on when it was your turn to go up on the watchtower.

Once again the convoy mixed the teams together and re-counted the Power-Station column by fives.

"The cold is worst at sun-up," the captain told the world. "It's the lowest point of night-time temperature loss."

The captain was fond of explaining things. Ask him and he'd work out for you whether the moon would be new or old on whatever day in whichever year you liked.

The captain was going downhill while you watched. His cheeks were sunken. But he kept his spirits up.

Outside camp the frost, with that nagging little wind blowing, nipped even Shukhov's case-hardened features painfully. Realising that it would be blowing in his face all the way to the Power Station he decided to put his facecloth on. He and many of the others had a bit of rag with two long strings to tie on when they were marched into the wind. The *zeks* found that it helped. He buried his face in it up to his eyes, drew the strings round over the lobes of his ears and tied them behind his head. Then he covered the back of his neck with the back flap of his cap and turned up his overcoat collar. Next he let down the front flap of his cap over his forehead. Seen from the front he was nothing but eyes. He drew the rope end tight round his jacket. Everything was fine now, except that his mittens were not much good and his hands were stiff with cold already. He rubbed them together and clapped them, knowing that any minute now he would have to put them behind his back and keep them there the whole way.

The escort commander recited the convict's daily "prayer" of which they were all heartily sick:

"Your attention, prisoners! Keep strictly to your column on the march! No spreading out, no running into the column in front, no moving from rank to rank, keep your eyes straight ahead, keep your hands behind your backs and nowhere else! One step to right or left will be considered an attempt to escape and the guards will open fire without warning! Leader – quick march!"

The two foremost guards marched off along the road. The column in front wavered, shoulders began swaying, and the guards twenty paces to right and left of the column, at intervals of ten paces, moved along, weapons at the ready.

The snow on the road was tight-packed and firm under foot – none had fallen for a week. As they rounded the camp, the wind hit their faces slantwise. Hands behind backs, heads lowered, the column moved off as if to a funeral. All you could see was the legs of the two or three men in front of you and the patch of trampled ground on which you were about to tread. From time to time a guard would yell: "Yu – forty! Hands behind you! B-five-o-two! Close up!" Then the shouts became less frequent: watchfulness wasn't easy in that cutting wind. The guards weren't allowed to tie rags around their faces, mind. Theirs wasn't much of a job either.

When it was a bit warmer they all talked on the march, however much they were yelled at. But today they kept their heads down, every man trying to shelter behind the man in front, and thought their own thoughts.

A convict's thoughts are no freer than he is: they come back to the same place, worry over the same thing continually. Will they poke around in my mattress and find my bread ration? Can I get off work if I report sick tonight? Will the captain be put in the hole or won't he? How did Tsezar get his hands on his warm vest? Must have greased somebody's palm in the storeroom, what else?

Because he had eaten only cold food, and gone without his bread ration at breakfast, Shukhov felt emptier than usual. To stop his belly mithering and begging for something to eat he put the camp out of his mind and started thinking about the letter he was shortly going to write home.

The column went past a woodworking plant (built by *zeks*), past a housing estate (*zeks* again had assembled these huts, but free workers lived in them), past the new recreation centre (all their own work, from the foundations to the murals – but it was the free workers who watched films there) and out onto the open steppe, walking into the wind and the reddening sunrise. Not so much as a sapling to be seen out on the steppe, nothing but bare white snow to left or right.

In the year just beginning – 1951 – Shukhov was entitled to write two letters. He had posted his last in July, and got an answer in October. In Ust-Izhma the rules had been different – you could write every month if you liked. But what was there to say? Shukhov hadn't written any more often than he did now.

He had left home on 23 June 1941. That Sunday people had come back from Mass in Polomnya and said "It's war." The post office there had heard the news – nobody in Temgenyovo had a radio before the war. Shukhov knew from letters that there was piped radio jabbering away in every cottage nowadays.

Writing letters now was like throwing stones into a bottomless pool. They sank without trace. No point in telling the family which gang you worked in and what

your foreman, Andrei Prokofievich Tyurin, was like.
Nowadays you had more to say to Kildigs, the Latvian,
than to the folk at home.

They wrote twice a year as well, and there was no way
in which he could understand how things were with
them. So the *kolkhoz* had a new chairman – well, it had a
new one every year, they never kept one any longer. So
the *kolkhoz* had been enlarged – well, they'd enlarged it
before and cut it down to size again. Then there was the
news that those not working the required number of days
had had their private plots trimmed to fifteen hundredths
of a hectare, or sometimes right up to the very house.
There was, his wife wrote, also a law that people could be
tried and put in jail for not working the norm, but that
law hadn't come into force for some reason.

One thing Shukhov couldn't take in at all was that,
from what his wife wrote, not a single living soul had
joined the *kolkhoz* since the war: all the young lads and
girls had somehow wangled their way to town to work in
a factory, or else to the peat workings. Half of the men
hadn't come back from the war, and those who had didn't
want anything to do with the *kolkhoz*: they just stayed at
home and did odd jobs. The only men on the farm were
the foreman Zakhar Vasilievich and the carpenter Tikhon,
who was eighty-four, but had married not long ago, and
had children. The *kolkhoz* was kept going by the women
who'd been herded into it back in 1930. When they
collapsed it would drop dead with them.

Try as he might, Shukhov couldn't understand the bit
about people living at home and working on the side. He
knew what it was to be a smallholder, and he knew what it
was to be in a *kolkhoz*, but living in the village and not
working in it was something he couldn't take in. Was it

like when the men used to hire themselves out for seasonal work? How did they manage with the haymaking?

But his wife told him that they'd given up hiring themselves out ages ago. They didn't travel round carpentering any more either – their part of the world was famous for its carpenters – and they'd given up making wicker baskets, there was no call for them. Instead there was a lively new trade – dyeing carpets. A demobbed soldier had brought some stencils home, and it had become all the rage. There were more of these master dyers all the time. They weren't on anybody's payroll, they had no regular job, they just put in a month on the farm, for haymaking and harvest, and got a certificate saying that *kolkhoz* member so-and-so had leave of absence for personal reasons and was not in arrears. So they went all round the country, they even flew in aeroplanes to save their precious time, and they raked the money in by the thousand, dyeing carpets all over the place. They charged fifty roubles to make a carpet out of an old sheet that nobody wanted, and it only took about an hour to paint the pattern on. His wife's dearest hope was that when he got home he would keep clear of the *kolkhoz* and take up dyeing himself. That way they could get out of the poverty she was struggling against, send their children to trade schools and build themselves a new cottage instead of their old tumble-down place. All the dyers were building themselves new houses. Down by the railway houses now cost twenty-five thousand instead of the five thousand they cost before.

Shukhov still had quite a bit of time to do – a winter, a summer, another winter, another summer – but all the same those carpets preyed on his mind. It could be just the job if he was deprived of rights or banished. So he asked his wife to tell him how he could be a dyer when he'd been no good at drawing from the day he was born. And anyway, what was so wonderful about these carpets? What was on them? She wrote back that any fool could make them. All you did was put the stencil on the cloth and rub paint through the holes. There were three sorts. There was the "Troika" – three horses in beautiful harness pulling a hussar officer – the "Stag", and one a bit like a Persian carpet. Those were the only patterns, but people all over the country jumped at the chance to buy them. Because a real carpet cost thousands of roubles, not fifty.

He wished he could get a squint at them.

In jail and in the camps Shukhov had lost the habit of scheming how he was going to feed his family from day to day or year to year. The bosses did all his thinking for him, and that somehow made life easier. But what would it be like when he got out?

He knew from what free workers said – drivers and bulldozer operators on construction sites – that the straight and narrow was barred to ordinary people, but they didn't let it get them down, they took a roundabout way and survived somehow.

Shukhov might have to do the same. It was easy money, and you couldn't miss. Besides, he'd feel pretty sore if others in the village got ahead of him. But still ... in his heart of hearts Shukhov didn't want to take up carpet-making. To do that sort of thing you had to be the free and easy type, you had to have plenty of cheek, and know when to grease a policeman's palm. Shukhov had been knocking around for forty years, he'd lost half his teeth and was going bald, but he'd never given or taken a bribe outside and hadn't picked up the habit in the camps.

Easy money had no weight: you didn't feel you'd earned it. What you get for a song you won't have for long, the old folks used to say, and they were right. He still had a good pair of hands, hands that could turn to anything, so what was to stop him getting a proper job on the outside?

Only – would they ever let him go? Maybe they'd slap another ten on him, just for fun?

By then the column had arrived, and halted at the guard house outside the sprawling work site. Two guards in sheepskin coats had fallen out at one corner of the boundary fence and were plodding to their distant watch-towers. Nobody would be allowed onto the site until the towers were manned. The escort commander made for the guardroom, with his weapon slung over his shoulder. Smoke was billowing out of the guardroom chimney: a free worker kept watch there all night to see that no one carried off planks and cement.

Looking through the wire gate, across the building site and out through the wire fence on the far side you could see the sun rising, big and red, as though in a fog. Alyoshka, standing next to Shukhov, gazed at the sun and a happy smile spread from his eyes to his lips. Alyoshka's cheeks were hollow, he lived on his bare ration and never made anything on the side – what had he got to be happy about? He and the other Baptists spent their Sundays whispering to each other. Life in the camp was like water off a duck's back to them. They'd been lumbered with twenty-five years a piece just for being Baptists. Fancy thinking that would cure them!

The facecloth he'd worn on the march was wet through from his breath, and a thick crust of ice had formed where the frost had caught it. Shukhov pulled it down from his face to his neck and turned his back on the wind. The cold hadn't really got through anywhere, only his hands felt the chill in those thin mittens, and the toes of his left foot were numb, because he'd burnt a hole in his felt boot and had to patch it twice.

He couldn't see himself doing much work with shooting pains in his midriff and all the way up his back.

He turned round and found himself looking at the foreman. He'd been marching in the last rank of five. Hefty shoulders, the foreman had, and a beefy face to match. Always looked glum. Not one to share a joke with the men, but kept them pretty well fed, saw to it they got good rations. A true son of the Gulag. On his second sentence, and he knew the drill inside out.

Your foreman matters more than anything else in a prison camp: a good one gives you a new lease of life, a bad one can land you in a wooden overcoat. Shukhov had known Andrei Prokofievich Tyurin back in Ust-Izhma. He hadn't worked under him there, but when all the "traitors" had been shunted from the ordinary penal camp to hard labour Tyurin had singled him out. Shukhov had no dealings with the camp commandant, the Production Planning Section, the site managers, or the engineers: his foreman was always in there standing up for him: a chest of steel, Tyurin had. But if he twitched an eyebrow or lifted a finger – you ran and did whatever he wanted. Cheat anybody you liked as long as you didn't cheat Tyurin, and you'd get by.

Shukhov wanted to ask the foreman whether they'd be working at the same place as yesterday or moving somewhere else, but didn't like to interrupt his lofty thoughts. Now he'd got Sotsgorodok off their backs, he'd be thinking about the rate for the job. The next five days' ration depended on it.

The foreman's face was deeply pock-marked. He didn't even squint when he stood looking into the wind. His skin was like the bark of an oak.

The men in the column were clapping their hands and stamping their feet. It was a nasty little wind. The poll-parrots must all be up on their perches by now, but the guards still wouldn't let the men in. They were overdoing the security.

At last! The guard commander came out of the guard house with the checker. They took their stand on opposite sides of the entrance and opened the gates.

"Sort yourselves out in fives! First five, second five."

The convicts marched off with something like a military step. Just let us in there, we'll do the rest!

Just past the guard house was the office shack. The site manager stood outside it urging the foremen to get a move on. They hardly needed to be told. Der, the *zek* they'd made an overseer, went with them. A real bastard, that one, treated his fellow *zeks* worse than dogs.

It was eight o'clock, no, five past eight already (that was the power-supply train hooting), and the bosses were afraid the *zeks* would scatter and waste time in cosy corners. A *zek's* day is a long one, though, and he can find time for everything. Every man entering the compound stooped to pick up a woodchip or two. Do nicely for our stove. Then quick as a flash into their boltholes.

Tyurin ordered Pavlo, the deputy foreman, to go with him into the office. Tsezar turned in there after them. Tsezar was rich, got two parcels a month, gave all the right people a hand-out, so he was a trusty, working in the office helping the norm-setter.*

The rest of Gang 104 scuttled out of sight.

A dim red sun had risen over the deserted compound: over prefab panels half-buried in snow drifts, over the brickwork of a building abandoned as soon as the founda-

*Represents interests of enterprise employing convict labour tions were laid, over the broken crank handle of an earth-moving machine, a jug, a heap of scrap iron. There were drains, trenches, holes everywhere. There were automobile repair shops in open-fronted sheds, and there, on a rise, stood the Power Station, its ground floor completed, its first floor just begun.

Everybody had gone into hiding, except for the six sentries on their towers and the group buzzing outside the office. This moment was the *zek's* very own! The senior site manager, so they said, was always threatening to give each gang its assignment the night before, but they could never make it work. Anything they decided at night would be stood on its head by morning.

Yes – this moment was their very own! While the bosses were getting organised – snuggle up in the warm, sit there as long as you can, you'll have a chance to break your back later, no need to hurry. The best thing was to get near a stove, and rewind your footrags (warm them a little bit first), so your feet would be warm all day. But even without a stove it was still pretty good.

Gang 104 went into the big auto-repair shop. Its windows had been installed in the autumn, and Gang 38 were working there, moulding concrete slabs. Some slabs were still in the moulds, some had been stood up on end, and there were piles of wire mesh lying around. The roof of the shop was high, and it had an earthen floor, so it would never be really warm, but still the big room was heated, and the bosses didn't spare the coal – not, of course, to keep the men warm, but to help the slabs set. There was even a thermometer hanging there, and if for some reason the camp didn't turn out to work on Sunday a free worker kept the stoves going.

Gang 38, of course, were blocking the stove, drying

their footrags, and wouldn't let outsiders anywhere near it. Never mind, it's not too bad up in the corner here.

Shukhov rested the shiny seat of his quilted trousers on the edge of a wooden mould and propped himself against the wall. As he leaned back his overcoat and jerkin tightened and he felt something hard pressing against the left side of his chest, near his heart. A corner of the crust in his inside pocket – the half of his morning ration he'd brought along for dinner. He always took that much to work and never touched it till dinner-time. But as a rule he ate the other half at breakfast, and this time he hadn't. So he hadn't really saved anything: he was dying to eat this portion right away while he was in the warm. It was five hours to dinner-time. A long haul.

The ache in his back had moved down to his legs now, and they suddenly felt weak. If only he could get up to the stove!

Shukhov placed his mittens on his knees, unbuttoned his jacket, untied his icy facecloth from round his neck, folded it a few times and tucked it in his pocket. Then he took out the piece of bread in the white rag and, holding it under his coat so that not a crumb would fall past the rag, began nibbling and chewing it bit by bit. He'd carried the bread under two layers of clothing, warming it with his body, so it wasn't the least bit frozen.

Since he'd been in the camps Shukhov had thought many a time of the food they used to eat in the village – whole frying pans full of potatoes, porridge by the cauldron, and, in the days before the *kolkhoz*, great hefty lumps of meat. Milk they used to lap up till their bellies were bursting. But he knew better now he'd been inside. He'd learnt to keep his whole mind on the food he was eating. Like now he was taking tiny little nibbles of bread,

softening it with his tongue, and drawing in his cheeks as
he sucked it. Dry black bread it was, but like that nothing
could be tastier. How much had he eaten in the last eight
or nine years? Nothing. And how hard had he worked?
Don't ask.

Shukhov, then, was busy with his two hundred
grammes, while the rest of Gang 104 made themselves
comfortable at the same end of the shop.

The two Estonians sat like two brothers on a low
concrete slab, sharing half a cigarette in a holder. They
were both tow-haired, both lanky, both skinny, they both
had long noses and big eyes. They clung together as
though neither would have air enough to breathe without
the other. The foreman never separated them. They
shared all their food and slept up top on the same bunk.
On the march, on work parade, or going to bed at night,
they never stopped talking to each other, in their slow
quiet way. Yet they weren't brothers at all – they'd met
for the first time in Gang 104. One of them, they
explained, was a Baltic fisherman, the other had been
taken off to Sweden by his parents when the Soviets were
set up. When he grew up he'd come back of his own free
will, silly idiot, to finish his education in the land of his
birth. He'd been pulled in the moment he arrived.

People said nationality didn't mean anything, that there
were good and bad in every nation. Shukhov had seen lots
of Estonians, and never come across a bad one.

There they all were, sitting on slabs, on moulds, on the
bare ground. Tongues were too stiff for talk in the
morning, so everybody withdrew into his own thoughts
and kept quiet. Fetyukov the scavenger had picked up a
lot of butt-ends (he'd even tip them out of the spittoon, he
wasn't squeamish). Now he was taking them apart on his
lap and sprinkling the half-burnt tobacco onto a single

piece of paper. Fetyukov had three children on the outside, but when he was jailed they'd all turned their backs on him, and his wife had married somebody else, so he got no help from anywhere.

Buynovsky kept looking sideways at him, and suddenly barked:

"Why do you pick up all that foul stuff? You'll get syphilis of the mouth before you know it! Chuck it away!"

The captain was used to giving orders. He talked to everybody like that.

But he had no hold over Fetyukov – he didn't get any parcels either. The scavenger gave a nasty little snigger – half his teeth were missing – and said:

"Just you wait, captain, when you've been inside eight years you'll be doing the same yourself."

True enough, the camp had seen off prouder people than Buynovsky in its time.

"Eh? What's that?" Senka Klevshin hadn't heard properly. He thought they'd been talking about Buynovsky's catching it on work parade that morning. "You'd have been all right if you hadn't flown off the handle," he said, shaking his head pityingly.

A quiet fellow, Senka Klevshin. One of the poor devil's ear drums had burst back in '41. Then he'd landed in a POW camp. Ran away three times. They'd caught up with him every time, and finally stuck him in Buchenwald. He'd escaped death by some miracle, and now he was serving his time quietly. Kick up a fuss, he said, and you're done for.

He was right there. Best to grin and bear it. Dig in your heels and they'll break you in two.

Alyoshka sat silent, with his face buried in his hands. Saying his prayers.

Shukhov nibbled his bread till his teeth met his fingers, but left a bit of the rounded upper crust: a piece of bread is better than any spoon for cleaning out a porridge bowl. He wrapped the crust in the white rag again till dinner-time, stuffed it into the pocket inside his jerkin, and buttoned himself up against the cold. Right – I'm ready for work as soon as they like to send me. Be nice if they hang about a bit longer, though.

Gang 38 got up and went their ways: some to the mixer, some to fetch water, some to collect wire mesh.

But neither Tyurin nor his deputy, Pavlo, had rejoined 104. And though the men had been sitting around for scarcely twenty minutes, and the working day (shortened in winter) would not end till six o'clock, they felt as happy as if it was nearly over. Kildigs, the plump, red-faced Latvian, sighed. "Long time since we had a blizzard! Not a single one all winter. What sort of winter is that?"

The gang all sighed for the blizzards they hadn't had.

When a blizzard blows up in those parts the bosses are afraid to take the men out of their huts, let alone to work. You can get lost on the way from your hut to the mess hall unless you sling a rope between them. If a convict dies out in the snow nobody gives a damn. But say he escapes. It has happened. In a blizzard the snow falls in tiny flakes, and the drifts are as firm as though packed by hand. Men have walked up such drifts straddling the wire and out of camp. Not that they ever got far.

When you come to think of it a blizzard is no use to anybody. The *zeks* sit under lock and key. Coal doesn't arrive on time, and the wind blows the warmth out of the hut. If no flour is delivered to the camp there'll be no bread. And however long the blizzard blows, whether it's three days or a week, every single day is counted as a day off, and the men are turned out to work Sunday after Sunday to make up for lost time.

All the same, *zeks* love blizzards and pray for them. As soon as the wind freshens they all throw their heads back and look at the sky:

"Come on, let's have the stuff! Let's have the stuff, then!"

Meaning snow.

A ground wind never works itself up into a decent blizzard.

A man tried to get warm at Gang 38's stove and was shooed away.

Then Tyurin came into the shop scowling. The team knew that there was work to be done and quickly.

"Right, then," Tyurin looked around. "All here, one-o-four?" Without stopping to check or count, because nobody ever tried to give him the slip, he began giving each man his job. The two Estonians, together with Klevshin and Gopchik, were sent to fetch a big mixing trough from nearby and carry it to the Power Station. This was enough to tell the gang that it was being switched to that building, which had been left half finished in late autumn. Two men were sent to the tool shop, where Pavlo was drawing the necessary tools. Four were assigned to snow clearance around the Power Station, at the entrance into the engine room itself, and on the ladder-walks. Another two were ordered to make a coal fire in the stove in the engine room – they'd have to pinch some boards and chop them up first. One man was to haul cement over on a sled. Two men would carry water, and two others sand. Another man would have to clear the snow away from the frozen sand and break it up with a crowbar.

This left only Shukhov and Kildigs – the most skilled men in the gang – without jobs. The foreman called them aside, and said "Listen, lads!" (He was no older than they were, but "lads" was a word he was always using.) "After dinner you'll be starting where Gang 61 left off last autumn, walling the second storey with breeze-blocks. But right now we must get the engine room warm. It's got three big windows, and your first job is to block them with something. I'll give you some men to help, you just think what you can use to board them up. We shall use the engine room for mixing, and to warm up in. If we don't get some heat into the place we'll freeze to death like dogs. Got it?"

He looked as if he had more to say, but Gopchik, a lad of about sixteen, as pink-cheeked as a piglet, came running to fetch him, complaining that another gang wouldn't let him have the mixing trough, and wanted to make a fight of it. So Tyurin shot off to deal with that.

It was hard starting a day's work in such cold, but that was all you had to do: make a start, and the rest was easy.

Shukhov and Kildigs looked at each other. They had worked as partners more than once before and the bricklayer and the carpenter respected each other's skills. Getting hold of something in the bare snow to stop up the windows wasn't going to be easy. But Kildigs said:

"Listen, Vanya! I know a place over by the prefabs where there's a big roll of tarred paper doing nothing. I tucked it away myself. Why don't we pop over?"

Though he was a Latvian Kildigs spoke Russian like a native – the people in the village next to his were Russians, Old Believers, and he'd learnt the language as a child. He'd been in the camps only two years, but he knew what was what: you get nothing by asking. Kildigs' name was Jan, and Shukhov called *him* Vanya too.

They decided to go for the tarred paper. But Shukhov hurried off first to pick up his trowel in the half-built wing of the auto-repair shop. It's very important to a bricklayer to have a trowel that's light and comfortable to hold. But the rule on every building site was collect all your tools in the morning, and hand them all back at night. And it was a matter of luck what sort of tools you'd get next day. So Shukhov had diddled the tool-maker out of a very good trowel one day. He hid it in a different place every time, and got it out in the morning if there was brick-laying to be done. Of course, if they'd been marched off to Sotsgorodok that morning he'd have been without a trowel again. But now he only had to shift a few pebbles and thrust his hand into the crevice – and out it came.

Shukhov and Kildigs left the auto-repair sheds and made for the prefabs. Their breath turned to dense steam as they walked. The sun was up now, but gave a dull blurry light as if through fog, and to either side of the sun stood – fence posts? Shukhov drew Kildigs' attention to them with a nod, but Kildigs dismissed it with a laugh.

"Fence posts won't bother us, as long as they don't string wire between them. That's what you've got to look out for."

Every word from Kildigs was a joke. The whole gang loved him for it. And the Latvians all over the camp had tremendous respect for him. But then, of course, Kildigs could count on a square meal, he got two parcels every month, he had colour in his cheeks and didn't look like a convict at all. He could afford to see the funny side.

Huge, their work site was, a country walk from one side to the other. They bumped into some lads from Gang 82 on the way. They'd been made to dig holes again. Not very big holes were needed – fifty centimetres by fifty, and fifty deep. But the ground was stone-hard even in summer, and it would take some tearing up now that the frost had a good hold. The pick-axe would glance off it, sparks would fly, but not a crumb of earth would be loosened. Each of the lads stood over a hole of his own, looking round now and then for somewhere to shelter. No, there was nowhere to go for a warm, and anyway they'd been forbidden to leave the spot, so they got to work with their picks again. That was all the warmth they'd be getting.

Shukhov saw a familiar face, a man from Vyatka, and offered him some advice.

"Here, what you diggers ought to do is light a fire over every hole. That way the ground would thaw out."

"They won't let us," the Vyatka man sighed. "Won't give us any firewood."

"So find some."

Kildigs spat in disgust.

"Come off it, Vanya, if the bosses had any brains d'you think they'd have people using pick-axes in weather like this?"

He added a few mumbled oaths and shut up. Nobody's very talkative when it's that cold. On and on they went till they reached the place where the prefab panels were buried under the snow.

Shukhov liked working with Kildigs, except for one thing – he didn't smoke, and there was never any tobacco in his parcels.

He had a sharp eye, though, Kildigs did: they helped each other to lift one board, then another, and underneath lay the roll of tarred paper.

They pulled it clear. The question now was how to carry it. It wouldn't matter if they were spotted from the watchtowers. The poll-parrots only worried about prisoners trying to run away. Inside the work area you could chop every last panel into splinters for all they cared. If a warder came by that wouldn't matter either: he'd be looking round for anything he could pick up himself. And no working convict gave a damn for those prefabs. Nor did the foremen. Only the site manager, a free employee, the *zek* supervisor and that gangling Shkuropatenko cared about them. Shkuropatenko was a nobody, just a *zek*, but he had the soul of a screw. He'd been put on a daily wage just to guard the prefabs and see that the *zeks* didn't make off with bits of them. Shkuropatenko was the one most likely to catch them out in the open there.

Shukhov had an idea.

"I tell you what, Vanya, we'd better not carry it flat. Let's stand it on end, put an arm each round it, and just walk steadily with it hidden between us. If he's not too close he'll be none the wiser."

It was a good idea. Getting an arm round the roll was awkward, though, so they just kept it pinned between them, like a third man, and moved off. From the side all you could see was two men walking shoulder to shoulder.

"The site manager will catch on anyway as soon as he sees tar-paper in the windows," Shukhov said.

Kildigs looked surprised. "So what's it got to do with us? When we turned up at the Power Station, there it was. Nobody could expect us to tear it down."

True enough.

Shukhov's fingers were frozen in those thin mittens, but his left boot was holding out. Boots were what mattered. Hands unstiffen once you start work.

They passed over a field of untrampled snow and came out onto a sled track leading from the tool shed to the Power Station. The cement must have been hauled along it.

The Power Station stood on a little hill, at the far end of the compound. Nobody had been near it for some time, and all the approaches were blanketed by a smooth layer of snow. The sled tracks, and a fresh trail of deep footprints, made by Gang 104, stood out all the more clearly. They were already at work with their wooden shovels, clearing a space round the plant and a path for the truck.

It would have been all right if the hoist had been working. But the engine had overheated and had never been fixed since. So they'd have to hump everything up to the second storey themselves. Not for the first time. Mortar. Breeze-blocks. The lot.

For two months the Power Station had stood abandoned, a grey skeleton out in the snow. But now Gang 104 had arrived. What kept body and soul together in these men was a mystery. Canvas belts were drawn tight round empty bellies. The frost was crackling merrily. Not a warm spot, not a spark of fire anywhere. All the same – Gang 104 had arrived, and life was beginning all over again.

The mortar trough lay in ruins right by the entrance to the generating room. It was a ramshackle thing. Shukhov had never had much hope that they'd get it there in one piece. The foreman swore a bit for the sake of appearances, but knew that nobody was to blame. Kildigs and Shukhov rolled in, frog-marching the tar-paper, just in time. The foreman brightened up and re-deployed his men: Shukhov would fix the chimney pipe to the stove so that they could light a fire quickly, Kildigs would mend the mortar trough, with the two Estonians to help him, Senka Klevshin would get busy with his axe: the tar-paper was only half the width of a window, and they needed laths to mount it on. But where would they come from?

The site manager wouldn't issue boards to make a warm-up room. The foreman looked around, they all looked around. There was only one thing for it. Knock off some of the boards attached for safety to the ramps up to the second storey. Nobody need fall off if he stepped warily. What else could they do?

Why, you may wonder, will a *zek* put up with ten years of back-breaking work in a camp? Why not say no and dawdle through the day? The night's his own.

It can't be done, though. The work gang was invented to take care of that. It isn't like a work gang outside, where Ivan Ivanovich and Pyotr Petrovich get each a wage of his own. In the camps things are arranged so that the *zek* is kept up to the mark not by his bosses but by the others in his gang. Either everybody gets a bonus or else they all die together. Am I supposed to starve because a louse like you won't work? Come on, you rotten bastard, put your back into it!

When a gang feels the pinch, as 104 did now, there's never any slacking. They jump to it, willy-nilly. If they didn't warm the place up in the next two hours, they'd all be done for, every last man.

Pavlo had brought the tools and Shukhov could help himself. There were a few lengths of piping as well, no tinsmith's tools, though. But there was a metal-worker's hammer and a hatchet. He'd manage somehow.

Shukhov clapped his mittened hands together, then began fitting pipes by hammering the ends into shape. More hand-clapping. More hammering. (His trowel was hidden not far away. The other men in the gang were his mates, but they could easily take it and leave him another. Kildigs was no different from the rest.)

Every other thought went clean out of his head. He had no memory, no concern for anything except how he was going to join the lengths of pipe and fix them so that the stove would not smoke. He sent Gopchik to look for wire, so that he could support the chimney where it stuck out through the window.

There was another stove, a squat one with a brick flue, over in the corner. Its iron tip got red-hot, and sand would thaw out and dry on it. This stove had already been lit, and the captain and Fetyukov were bringing in sand in a handbarrow. You don't need brains to carry a hand-barrow. That's why the foreman had put these ex-bosses on the job. Fetyukov was supposed to have been a big boss in some office. Went around in a car.

When they first worked together Fetyukov had tried throwing his weight about and shouting at the captain. But the captain smacked him in the teeth, and they called it quits.

Some of the lads were sidling up to the stove with the sand on it, hoping for a warm, but the foreman warned them off.

"I'll warm one or two of you with my fist in a minute! Get the place fixed up first!"

One look at the whip is enough for a beaten dog! The cold was fierce, but the foreman was fiercer. The lads went back to their jobs.

Shukhov heard the foreman speak quietly to Pavlo:

"You hang on here and keep a tight hold on things. I've got to go and see about the percentages."

More depends on the percentages than the work itself. A foreman with any brains concentrates more on the percentages than on the work. It's the percentage that feeds us. Make it look as if the work's done, whether it is or not. If the rate for the job is low wangle things so that it turns out dearer. That's what a foreman needs a big brain for. And an understanding with the norm-setters. The norm-setters have their hands out too.

Just think, though – who benefits from all this overful-filment of norms? The camp does. The camp rakes in thousands extra from a building job and awards prizes to its lieutenants. To Volkovoy, say, for that whip of his. All *you*'ll get is an extra two hundred grammes of bread of an evening. But your life can depend on those two hundred grammes. Two-hundred-gramme portions built the Belo-mor★ Canal.

Two buckets of water had been brought in, but they'd iced over on the way. Pavlo decided that there was no point in fetching any more. Quicker to melt snow on the spot. They stood the buckets on the stove.

Gopchik, who had pinched some new aluminium wire, the sort electricians use, had something to say:

"Hey, Ivan Denisovich! Here's some good wire for spoons. Will you show me how to mould one?"

Ivan Denisovich was fond of Gopchik, the rascal (his own son had died when he was little, and he only had two grown-up daughters at home). Gopchik had been jailed for taking milk to Ukrainian guerrillas hiding in the forest. They'd given him a grown-up's sentence. He fussed around the prisoners like a sloppy little calf. But he was crafty enough: kept his parcels to himself. You sometimes heard him munching in the middle of the night.

Well, there wouldn't have been enough to go round.

They broke off enough wire for spoons and hid it in a corner. Shukhov rigged up a sort of ladder from two planks and sent Gopchik up to attach the chimney pipe.

★Baltic–White Sea Canal built 1931–3 at great human cost by convict labour

Gopchik was as light as a squirrel. He scrambled over the crossbeams, knocked in a nail, slung the wire over it and looped it round the pipe. Shukhov had not been idle: he had finished the chimney with an elbow pipe pointing upwards. There was no wind, but there would be tomorrow, and he didn't want the smoke to blow down. They were fixing this stove for themselves, remember.

By then Senka Klevshin had split off some long strips of wood. They made Gopchik nail on the tarred paper. He scrambled up, the little imp, calling down to them as he went.

The sun had hoisted itself higher and driven the mist away. The "posts" to either side of it were no longer visible, just the deep red glow between.

They had got the stove going with stolen firewood. Made things a lot more cheerful.

"In January the sun warmed the cow's flanks," Shukhov commented.

Kildigs had finished knocking the mortar trough together. He gave a final tap with his axe and called out: "Hey Pavlo, I want a hundred from the foreman for this job, I won't take a copeck less."

"You might get a hundred grammes," Pavlo said, laughing.

"With a bonus from the prosecutor," Gopchik shouted from aloft.

"Don't touch it! Leave it alone," yelled Shukhov suddenly. They were cutting the tarred paper the wrong way. He showed them how to do it.

Men had flocked round the tin stove, but Pavlo chased them away. He gave Kildigs some helpers and told him to make hods – they'd need them to get the mortar up above. He put a few extra men on fetching sand. Others were sent aloft to clear snow from the scaffolding and the brickwork itself. Another man, inside the building, was told to take the hot sand from the stove and tip it into the mortar trough.

An engine roared outside. They'd started bringing breeze-blocks, and the truck was trying to get up close. Pavlo dashed out waving his arms to show them where to dump the load.

By now they'd nailed on one width of tar-paper, then a second. What sort of protection would it give though? Tarred or not, it was still just paper. Still, it looked like some sort of solid screen. And made it darker inside so that the stove burned brighter.

Alyoshka had brought coal. "Chuck it on!" some of them yelled, but others said "Don't! We'll be warmer with just wood!" He stood still, wondering which lot to obey.

Fetyukov had settled down by the stove and was shoving his felt boots – the idiot! – almost into the fire. The captain yanked him up by the scruff of his neck and gave him a push in the direction of the handbarrow.

"Go and fetch sand, you feeble bastard!"

The captain saw no difference between work in a camp and work on shipboard. Orders were orders! He'd got very haggard in the last month, the captain had, but he was still a willing horse.

Before too long they had all three windows curtained with tar-paper. The only light now came through the doors. And the cold came in with it. Pavlo ordered them to board up the upper part of the door space and leave the bottom so that a man could get in, stooping. The job was done.

Meanwhile three truck-loads of breeze-blocks had been delivered and dumped. The question now was how to get them up to the second storey without a hoist.

"Come on men, let's get on with it!" Pavlo called to the bricklayers.

It was a job to take pride in. Shukhov and Kildigs went up after Pavlo. The ramp was narrow enough to begin with, and now that Senka had broken off the handrail you had to hug the wall if you didn't want to land on your head. Worse still, snow had frozen onto the slats and made them round, so that there was no good foothold. How were they going to get the mortar up?

They took a look at the half-finished walls. Men were already shovelling snow from them, but would have to chip the ice from the old courses with hatchets and sweep it clear.

They worked out where they wanted the breeze-blocks handed up, then took a look down. That was it – they'd station four men below to heave them onto the lower scaffolding, another two there to pass them up, and another two on the second floor to feed the bricklayers. That would still be quicker than lugging the things up the ramp.

On top the wind wasn't strong, but it never let up. It'll blow right through us, Shukhov thought, when we start laying. Still, if we shelter behind the part that's done already it'll be warmer, not too bad at all.

He looked up at the sky and gasped: it had cleared and the sun was nearly high enough for dinner-time. Amazing how time flew when you were working. He'd often noticed that days in the camp rolled by before you knew it. Yet your sentence stood still, the time you had to serve never got any less.

They went back down and found the rest all sitting round the stove, except for the captain and Fetyukov, who were still carrying sand. Pavlo lost his temper, chased eight men off to shift breeze-blocks, ordered two to pour cement into the mortar trough and dry-mix it with sand, sent one for water and another for coal. Kildigs turned to his detachment: "Right boys, we've got to finish this handbarrow."

Shukhov was looking for work. "Should I give them a hand?" he asked.

Pavlo nodded. "Do that."

A tub was brought in to melt snow for mortar. They heard somebody saying it was twelve o'clock already.

"It's sure to be twelve," Shukhov announced. "The sun's over the top already."

"If it is," the captain retorted, "it's one o'clock, not twelve."

"How do you make that out?" Shukhov asked in surprise. "The old folk say the sun is highest at dinner-time."

"Maybe it was in their day!" the captain snapped back. "Since then it's been decreed that the sun is highest at one o'clock."

"Who decreed that?"

"The Soviet government."

The captain took off with the handbarrow, but Shukhov wasn't going to argue anyway. As if the sun would obey their decrees!

A few more bangs, a few more taps and they had knocked four hods together.

"Right, let's sit down and have a warm," Pavlo said to the two bricklayers. "You as well, Senka – you'll be laying after dinner. Sit!"

So they got to sit by the stove lawfully. They couldn't start laying before dinner anyway, and if they mixed the mortar too soon it would only freeze.

The coal had begun to glow and was giving off a steady heat. But you could only feel it by the stove. The rest of the room was as cold as ever.

All four of them took off their mittens and wagged their hands at the stove.

But – a word to the wise – don't ever put your feet near a fire when you're wearing boots or shoes. If they're leather shoes they'll crack, and if they're felt boots they'll steam and get damp and you won't be the least bit warmer. And if you hold them any nearer you'll burn them. And you won't get another pair, so you'll be tramping around in leaky boots till next spring.

"Shukhov's all right, though," Kildigs said, teasing him. "Know what, boys? He's got one foot through his own front door already."

Somebody took up the joke.

"Right, that foot, the bare one." They all burst out laughing.

(Shukhov had taken the burnt left boot off to warm his footrag.)

"Shukhov's nearly done his time," Kildigs said.

He himself was serving twenty-five years. In happier days everybody got a flat ten. But in '49 a new phase set in: everybody got twenty-five regardless. Ten you could just about do without turning up your toes. But twenty-five?

Shukhov enjoyed it. He liked people pointing at him – see that man? He's nearly done his time – but he didn't let himself get excited about it. Those who'd come to the end of their time during the war had all been kept in "pending further orders" – till '46. So people originally sentenced to three years did five altogether. They could twist the law any way they liked. When your ten years were up they could say good, have another ten. Or pack you off to some Godforsaken place of exile.

Sometimes, though, you got thinking and your spirits soared: your sentence was running out, there wasn't much thread left on the spool! Lord! Just to think of it! Walking free, on your own two legs!

But it wouldn't be nice to say such things out loud to one of the old inhabitants. So Shukhov said to Kildigs:

"Don't keep counting. Who knows whether you'll be here twenty-five years or not? Guessing is like forking water. All I know for sure is I've done a good eight."

When you're flat on your face there's no time to wonder how you got in and when you'll get out.

According to his dossier Shukhov was in for treason. He'd admitted it under investigation – yes, he had surrendered in order to betray his country, and returned from POW camp to carry out a mission for German intelligence. What the mission could be neither Shukhov himself nor his interrogator could imagine. They left it at that – just "a mission".

The counter-espionage boys had beaten the hell out of him. The choice was simple enough: don't sign and wear a wooden overcoat, or sign and live a bit longer.

He signed.

What had really happened was this. In February '42 the whole North-Western army was surrounded. No grub was being dropped by planes, and there were no planes anyway. It got so bad they were filing the hooves of dead horses, sousing the horny shavings in water and eating them. They had no ammunition either. So the Germans rounded them up a few at a time in the forest. Shukhov was a prisoner in one such group for a couple of days, then he and four others escaped. They crawled about in the woods and marshes till they found themselves by some miracle among friends. True, a friendly tommy-gunner stretched two of them, and a third died from his wounds, so only two of them made it. If they'd had any sense they'd have said they'd got lost in the forest, and nothing would have happened to them. But they came out in the open; yes, we were taken prisoner, we've escaped from the Germans. Escaped prisoners, eh? Like fuck you are! Nazi spies, more like! Behind bars is where you belong. Maybe if there'd still been five of them their statements would have been compared and believed. Just the two of them hadn't a chance: these two bastards have obviously worked out this escape story of theirs together.

Senka Klevshin made out through his deafness some talk about escaping and said loudly:

"I've escaped three times and been caught three times."

The long-suffering Senka was mostly silent. Couldn't hear and didn't butt in. So nobody knew much about him except that he'd gone through Buchenwald, been in an underground organisation there, and carried weapons into the compound for an uprising. And that the Germans had tied his hands behind his back, strung him up by his wrists, and thrashed him with canes.

Kildigs felt like arguing.

"So you've done eight, Vanya," he said, "but what sort of camps were you in? Ordinary camps, sleeping with women. You didn't wear numbers. Just you try eight years' hard. Nobody's gone the distance yet."

"Women! Sleeping with logs, I was!" Shukhov stared into the flames and his seven years in the north came back to him. Three years hauling logs for crates and rail-ties to the log-slide. The camp-fire at the felling site was just like this one – now you saw it, now you didn't – and that was on night shift, not in the daytime. The big boss had laid down a law: any gang that didn't fulfil its daily quota stayed on after dark.

It would be past midnight when they dragged themselves back to camp, and they'd be off to the forest again next morning.

"No, friends," he lisped, "if you ask me, it's more peaceful here. We knock off on time — that's the law. Perhaps you've done your stint, perhaps you haven't, but it's back to the camp at quitting time. And the guaranteed ration is a hundred grammes more. Life isn't so bad here. All right — it's a special camp. But why does wearing numbers bother you? They weigh nothing, number patches."

"More peaceful!" Fetyukov hissed. (It was getting near the dinner-break, and they'd all found their way to the stove.) "People are getting their throats cut in bed. And he says it's more peaceful!"

Pavlo raised a threatening finger at Fetyukov. "Stoolies, not people."

It was true. Something new had started happening in the camp. Two known stool pigeons had had their throats slit at getting-up time. Then the same had happened to an innocent working prisoner — whoever did it must have got the wrong bed. One stoolie had run off to the stone jail house for safety, and the bosses had hidden him there. Queer goings on. There'd never been anything like it in ordinary criminal camps. But then it never used to happen in this one.

The power-train's hooter suddenly blared. Not at the top of its voice to begin with, but with a hoarse rasping noise as though clearing its throat.

"Mid-day! Down tools! Dinner-break!"

Damn, we've missed our chance! Should have gone to the mess and queued up a while ago.

There were eleven gangs at the site, and the mess would only hold two at a time.

The foreman still wasn't back: Pavlo took a quick look around and made up his mind.

"Shukhov and Gopchik – come with me. Kildigs – when I send Gopchik back bring the team over right away."

Their places at the stove were grabbed immediately. Men hovered round that stove as though it was a woman they wanted to get their hands on.

There were shouts of "Wake up, somebody! Get your fags out!"

They looked at each other to see who would light up. Nobody was going to. Either they had no tobacco or they were keeping it to themselves.

Shukhov went outside with Pavlo. Gopchik hopped along behind like a little rabbit.

"It's warmed up a bit," Shukhov decided. "Eighteen below, no more. Good weather for bricklaying."

They turned to look at the breeze-blocks. The lads had already dumped a lot of them on the scaffolding, and heaved some up to the planking on the second floor.

Shukhov squinted into the sun, checking out what the captain had said about the decree.

Out in the open where the wind had plenty of room it still nagged and nipped. Just in case they forgot it was January.

The work site cook house was a little matchwood hovel tacked together round a stove and faced with rusty tinplates to hide the cracks. Inside, a partition divided it into kitchen and eating area. The floors in kitchen and mess room alike were bare earth, churned up by feet and frozen into holes and hillocks. The kitchen was just a square stove with a cauldron cemented onto it.

Two men operated the kitchen – a cook and a hygienist. The cook was given a supply of meal in the big kitchen before leaving camp in the morning. Maybe fifty grammes a head, a kilo for every gang, say a bit less than a *pood* for the whole site. The cook wasn't going to carry a sack of meal that heavy for three kilometres so he let his stooge do it. Better to give the stooge a bit extra out of the workers' rations than to break your own back.

There were other jobs the cook wouldn't do for himself, like fetching water and firewood, and lighting the stove. These too were done by other people, workers or goners, and the cook gave each of them an extra portion, he didn't grudge what wasn't his own. Then again, men weren't supposed to take food out of the mess. Bowls had to be brought from camp (you couldn't leave them on the site overnight or the free workers would pinch them), and they brought only fifty, which had to be washed and passed on quickly. So the man who carried the bowls also had to be given an extra portion. Yet another stooge was posted at the door to see that bowls weren't carried out. But however watchful he was, people would distract his attention or talk their way past him. So somebody had to be sent round the site collecting dirty bowls and bringing them back to the kitchen. The doorman got an extra portion. And so did the collector.

All the cook had to do was sprinkle meal and salt into the cauldron and divide the fat into two parts, one for the pot and one for himself. (Good fat never found its way to the workers, the bad stuff went straight into the pot. So the *zeks* were happier when the stores issued bad fat.) Next, he stirred the gruel as it thickened. The hygienist★ did even less – just sat and watched. When the gruel was

★ *Zek* with no special training, appointed to represent camp hospital cooked he was the first to be served: eat all your belly can hold. The cook did likewise. Then the duty foreman would come along – they took it in turn, a day at a time – to sample the stuff and make sure it was fit for the workers to eat. He got a double portion for his efforts. And would eat again with his gang.

The hooter sounded. The work gangs arrived one after another, and the cook passed bowls through his hatch. The bottom of each bowl was covered with watery gruel. No good asking or trying to weigh how much of your meal ration you were getting: they'd make it hot for you if you let out a peep.

The wind whistles over the bare steppe – hot and dry in summer, freezing in winter. Nothing has ever been known to grow on that steppe, least of all between four barbed-wire fences. Wheat sprouts only in the bread-cutting room, oats put out ears only in the foodstore. Break your back working, grovel on the ground, you'll cudgel never a scrap of food out of it. What the bossman doles out is all you will get. Only you won't get even that, what with cooks and their stooges and trusties. There's thieving on the site, there's thieving in the camp, and there was thieving before the food ever left the store. And not one of these thieves wields a pick-axe himself. You do that, and take what you're given. And move away from the serving hatch.

It's dog eat dog here.

When Pavlo entered the mess with Shukhov and Gopchik men were standing on one another's feet – you couldn't see the sawn-off tables and benches for them. Some ate sitting down, but most of them standing. Gang 82, which had been sinking holes for fence posts all morning without a warm, had grabbed the first places as soon as the hooter went. Now even those who'd finished eating wouldn't move. They had nowhere to go. The others cursed them, but it was water off a duck's back – anything is more fun than being out in the freezing cold.

Pavlo and Shukhov elbowed their way through. They'd come at a good time. One gang was just being served, there was only one other in the queue. Their deputy foremen were standing at the hatch. So all the other gangs would be behind 104.

"Bowls! Bowls!" the cook shouted from his hatch.

Bowls were passed through. Shukhov collected a few himself and shoved them at him – not in the hope of getting more gruel but just to speed things up.

The stooges were washing bowls behind the screen – in return for more gruel.

The deputy foreman in front of Pavlo was about to be served. Pavlo shouted over the heads around him.

"Gopchik!"

"Here!" The thin little voice like the bleat of a goat came from near the door.

"Call the gang."

Gopchik ran off.

The great news was that the gruel was good today, the very best, oatmeal gruel. You don't often get that. It's usually magara or grits twice a day. The mushy stuff round the grains of oatmeal is filling, it's precious.

Shukhov had fed any amount of oats to horses as a youngster, and never thought that one day he'd be breaking his heart for a handful of the stuff.

"Bowls! Bowls!" came a shout from the serving hatch.

One-o-four's turn was coming. The deputy foreman up front took a double foreman's portion and stopped blocking the hatch.

This was also at the workers' expense – and yet again nobody quibbled. Every foreman got the same, and could eat it himself or pass it on to his assistant. Tyurin gave his extra portion to Pavlo.

Shukhov had his work cut out. He squeezed in at the table, shooed two goners away, asked one worker nicely, and made room for twelve bowls placed close together, with a second tier of six, and another two right on top. Then he had to take the bowls from Pavlo, check the count, and make sure no outsider rustled one from the table. Or jostled him and upset one. Meanwhile other men were scrambling onto or off the bench, or sitting there eating. You had to keep an eye on your territory to make sure they were eating from their own bowls, not dipping into yours.

"Two, four, six," the cook counted behind his hatch. He handed two bowls at a time into two outstretched hands. One at a time might confuse him.

"Two! Four! Six!" Pavlo echoed in a low voice on the other side of the hatch, quickly passing two bowls at a time to Shukhov, who placed them on the table. Shukhov said nothing out loud, but kept a closer count than either of them.

"Eight, ten."

Where was Kildigs with the gang?

The count went on. "Twelve, fourteen!"

They'd run out of bowls in the kitchen. Shukhov saw, over Pavlo's shoulder, the cook's two hands put two bowls on the counter and pause while he thought. He must have turned his head to curse the dishwashers. At that moment someone shoved a stack of emptied bowls through the hatch at him, and he took his hands off the bowls on the counter while he passed the empties back.

Shukhov abandoned the stack of bowls already on the table, stepped nimbly over the bench, whisked the two bowls from the counter, and repeated, not very loudly, as though it was meant for Pavlo, not the cook:

"Fourteen."

"Hold it! Where are you going with those?" the cook bellowed.

"He's my man, take it easy."

"All right, but don't try muddling the count."

"It's fourteen," said Pavlo with a shrug. He'd never swipe an odd bowl himself, as deputy foreman he had to uphold authority, but this time he was only repeating what Shukhov had said and could blame him.

"I said fourteen before!" the cook said furiously.

"So what?" Shukhov yelled. "You said fourteen but you didn't hand 'em over, you never let go of 'em. Come and count if you don't believe me. They're all here on the table.

He could shout at the cook because he'd noticed the two Estonians pushing their way through to him, and shoved the two bowls into their hands as they came. He also managed to get back to the table and to do a quick count – yes, they were all there, the neighbours hadn't got round to pinching any, though there was nothing to stop them.

The cook's red moonface appeared in close-up through the hatch.

"Where are the bowls?" he asked sternly.

"Look for yourself," Shukhov shouted. He gave somebody a push. "Out of the way, big boy, don't block the view. Here's two" – he raised the two second-storey bowls an inch – "and there's three rows of four, dead right, count them."

"Your gang not here yet?" The cook was staring suspiciously through the small opening. The hatch had been made narrow so that people couldn't peep through from the dining room and see how much was left in the cauldron.

Pavlo shook his head. "No, they're not here yet."

"So what the hell d'you mean by it, hogging bowls before the gang gets here?" The cook was beside himself with rage.

"Here they come now!" Shukhov shouted. They could all hear the captain barking in the doorway as though he was still on the bridge of his ship.

"Must you clutter up the place like this? Eat up, get out and give somebody else a chance."

The cook growled a bit more, then his face disappeared and his hands appeared at the hatch again.

"Sixteen, eighteen ..." and, as he poured the last portion, a double one, "twenty-three! That's the lot! Next gang!"

As the gang shoved their way through, Pavlo passed the bowls, some of them over the heads of men already seated, to a second table.

In summer they could sit five to a bench, but now they were all wearing such bulky clothes that there was hardly room for four, and even they had a job to use their spoons.

Taking it for granted that one of the bowls he'd swiped would be his, Shukhov quickly set about the one he'd earned in the sweat of his brow. This meant drawing his right knee up to his belly, unsheathing his "Ust-Izhma 1944" spoon from the leg of his boot, removing his cap and tucking it under his left arm, and running his spoon round the rim of the bowl.

This minute should have been one of concentration on the business of eating – spooning the thin layer of gruel from the bottom of the bowl, cautiously raising it to his mouth and rolling it around with his tongue. But he had to hurry, so that Pavlo would see him finish and offer him the second portion. And then there was Fetyukov, who had arrived with the Estonians and had spotted him swiping the two bowls, and was now eating on his feet across the table from Pavlo, ogling the gang's four unallotted portions. This was a hint that he too expected a half-portion if not a full one.

But Pavlo went on calmly eating his own double portion, and there was no knowing from the look on his swarthy young face whether he was aware of Fetyukov and remembered the two extra portions.

Shukhov had finished his gruel. Because his belly had been agape for two portions at once it felt less full than usual after oatmeal. He reached into his inside pocket, took his unfrozen piece of round crust out of the offwhite rag, and carefully mopped the last remains of the oatmeal smear from the bottom and sloping sides of the bowl. When he had collected enough he licked the gruel from the crust and mopped up as much again. In the end the bowl was as clean as if it had been washed, except for a faint film. He passed it over his shoulder to the collector and sat a minute longer with his hat off.

It was Shukhov who had swiped the extra bowls, but the deputy foreman could do what he liked with them.

Pavlo tantalised him a bit longer while he finished his gruel, licked his spoon clean (but not the bowl), put it away safely and crossed himself. Then he gave two of the four bowls a bit of a push – he was hemmed in too tightly to pass them – surrendering them to Shukhov.

"One for you, Ivan Denisovich, and one for Tsezar."

Shukhov hadn't forgotten that he would have to take one bowl to the office for Tsezar, who never lowered himself by coming to the mess, either on the site or in camp. But when Pavlo touched the two bowls at once

his heart stood still: was he giving them both to Tsezar?
Now his pulse was normal again.

He crouched over his lawful spoil and ate thoughtfully,
taking no notice of the newly arrived gangs shoving past
behind him. His one worry was that Fetyukov might get a
second bowl. Fetyukov hadn't the nerve to swipe anything for himself but he was a champion scrounger.

Buynovsky was sitting a little way along the table. He
had finished his gruel some time ago, didn't know that
104 had extra portions, and hadn't looked to see how
many the deputy foreman had left. He had grown
sluggish as he warmed up, and hadn't the strength to rise
and go out into the cold air or to the chilly "warming
shed" that warmed nobody. Now he was behaving
like those he had tried to drive away with his metallic
voice five minutes ago – taking up space to which he
was not entitled and getting in the way of the gangs just
arriving. He was new to camp life and to general duties.
Moments like this, though he didn't know it, were very
important to him: they were turning the loud and domi-
neering naval officer into a slow-moving and circumspect
zek: only this economy of effort would enable him to
endure the twenty-five years of imprisonment doled out
to him.

People were pushing him from behind and yelling at
him to give up his seat.

Pavlo spoke to him. "Captain! You there, Captain?"

Buynovsky started as if waking from a doze and looked
round.

Pavlo held out the bowl of gruel without asking
whether he wanted it.

Buynovsky's eyebrows rose, and he stared at the gruel
as though it was an unheard-of miracle.

"Go on, take it," Pavlo said reassuringly, then picked up the last bowl and carried it off to the foreman.

A guilty smile parted the captain's chapped lips. He had sailed all round Europe and across the Great Northern Sea Route, but now he bowed his head happily over less than a ladleful of thin gruel with no fat in it at all, just oats and water.

Fetyukov gave Shukhov and the captain an evil look and went out.

Shukhov himself thought it only right that the captain should get the spare portion. He might learn to look after himself some day, but so far he had no idea.

Shukhov also had some faint hope that Tsezar would hand over his gruel. Though he had no call to, because he hadn't had a parcel for two weeks.

After his second portion Shukhov mopped the bottom and sides of the bowl, sucking his crust each time, as before, then finished off the crust itself. After which he picked up Tsezar's stone-cold gruel and left the mess.

"For the office," he said, pushing aside the stooge on the door, who didn't want to let him out with a bowl.

The office was a log cabin near the guard house. Smoke was still pouring from its chimney, as it had all morning. An orderly who also acted as their messenger kept the fire going. He was paid by the hour. The office was allowed any amount of kindling and firewood.

Shukhov opened a creaking door into a little lobby, then another door padded with oakum, and entered with a rush of frosty air, pulling the door to before anybody could shout "Shut it, clod!"

The office seemed to him as hot as a bath house. From the top of the Power Station the sun had looked cold and unfriendly: here it sparkled cheerfully through windows

from which the ice was melting. Clouds of smoke from
Tsezar's pipe floated in the sunlight like incense in church.
The whole stove was aglow – the thickheads had got it
red-hot. The chimney pipe was red-hot too.

Sit down for a minute in that heat and you'd be fast
asleep.

The office had two rooms. The door to the second, the
site manager's room, was slightly ajar, and he was
thundering:

"We're overspent on wages and we're overspent on
building materials. Prisoners chop up expensive boards,
and I don't mean just prefab panels, for firewood to burn
in their shelters, and you turn a blind eye. The other day
some prisoners were unloading cement outside the stores
in a high wind and carrying it as much as ten metres on
handbarrows, so the whole area round the stores was ankle
deep in the stuff and the workers left the site in grey
instead of black. It's waste, waste, waste all the time!"

The manager was evidently in conference. With the
overseers no doubt.

A stupefied orderly was sitting on a stool in a corner by
the entrance. Beyond him, Shkuropatenko, prisoner
B-219, a crooked beanpole of a man, was staring through
the window with his wall-eye, still trying to make out
whether anybody was pinching his prefabs. The old fool
had seen the last of his tar-paper anyway.

Two book-keepers, also *zeks*, were toasting bread on
the stove. They'd rigged up a sort of wire griddle to keep
it from burning.

Tsezar was lolling at his desk smoking his pipe. He had
his back to Shukhov and didn't see him.

Opposite him sat Kh-123, a tough old boy doing
twenty years hard. He was eating gruel.

"You're wrong, old man," Tsezar was saying, good-naturedly. "Objectively you are bound to admit that Eisenstein is a genius. Surely you can't deny that *Ivan the Terrible* is a work of genius? The dance of the masked *oprichniki*! The scene in the cathedral!"

Kh-123's spoon stopped short of his mouth.

"Bogus," he said angrily. "So much art in it that it ceases to be art. Pepper and poppy-seed instead of good honest bread. And the political motive behind it is utterly loathsome – an attempt to justify a tyrannical individual. An insult to the memory of three generations of the Russian intelligentsia!" (He was eating his gruel without savouring it. It wouldn't do him any good.)

"But would it have got past the censor if he'd handled it differently?"

"Oh well, if that's what matters . . . Only don't call him a genius – call him a toady, a dog carrying out his master's orders. A genius doesn't adjust his treatment of a theme to a tyrant's taste."

"Ahem!" Shukhov cleared his throat. He felt awkward interrupting this educated conversation, but he couldn't just go on standing there.

Tsezar turned round and held his hand out for the bowl, without even looking at Shukhov (the gruel might have travelled through the air unaided) then went back to his argument.

"Yes, but art isn't what you do, it's how you do it."

Kh-123 reared up and chopped at the table with his hand.

"I don't give a damn how you do it if it doesn't awaken good feelings in me!"

Shukhov stood there just as long as he decently could after handing over the gruel, hoping Tsezar would treat him to a cigarette. But Tsezar had entirely forgotten that Shukhov was behind him. So he turned on his heel and left quietly.

Never mind, it wasn't all that cold outside. A great day for bricklaying.

Walking down the path he spotted a bit of steel broken off a hacksaw blade lying in the snow. He had no special use for it right then, but you never knew what you might need later. So he picked it up and slipped it into his trouser pocket. Have to hide it in the Power Station. Thrift beats riches.

The first thing he did when he got back to the Power Station was find his trowel and shove it under the rope round his waist. Then he dived into the mortar-mixing room.

Coming in from the sun he found it quite dark, and no warmer than outside. The air was if anything rawer. Men huddled close to the round stove rigged up by Shukhov, and the other stove on which thawing sand was steaming. Those for whom there was no room sat on the edge of the mixing trough. The foreman sat right by the fire eating the last of his gruel. Pavlo had warmed it up for him on the stove.

A lot of whispering was going on, and the lads were looking more cheerful. Somebody quietly gave Ivan Denisovich the news: the foreman had got a good rate for the job and come back all smiles.

What work he could point to so far only he knew. Half the day was gone and they'd done nothing. They wouldn't be paid for rigging up a stove and making themselves a warm shelter: that was work for themselves not for the site. Something would have to be entered on the worksheet. Maybe Tsezar would slip in a few extras to oblige the foreman. The foreman treated Tsezar with respect, and he must have some reason for it.

"A good rate for the job" meant good rations for five days. Well, four days more likely: the bosses would claw back one day's rations and hand out the minimum to every gang in the camp, good or bad. Fair shares all round they called it – fair to everybody, but they were saving at the expense of the *zek's* belly. Of course a *zek's* stomach can put up with anything: if today's no good we'll stuff ourselves tomorrow. That was the dream the whole camp went to bed with on minimum-ration days.

Just think though – it was five days' work and four days' eats.

The gang made little noise. Those who had tobacco took a few sly drags. Stared at the fire, huddled together in the half dark. Like a big family. That's what a work gang is – a family. They could hear the foreman yarning to two or three others near the stove. He never wasted words. If he was telling the tale he must be in a good mood.

Andrei Petrovich Tyurin, the foreman, was another who hadn't learned to eat with his cap on. Without it his head was an old man's. It was close-cropped, like everyone else's, and you could see in the firelight a sprinkling of white hairs amongst the grey.

"I was scared even of the battalion commander, and this was the CO. 'Private Tyurin, reporting for orders,' I say. He fixes me with a stare from under his shaggy eyebrows and says 'Name and patronymic?' I tell him. 'Year of birth?' I tell him. Well, what was I in 1930, I was all of twenty-two, just a pup. 'And who are you here to serve, Tyurin?' 'I serve the toiling people.' He boils over and bangs the desk with both hands. 'The toiling people! And what do you call yourself, you rotter?' It was like I'd swallowed something scalding. 'Machine gunner, first class,' I say. 'Passed out with distinction in military and political subjects.' 'First class, you vermin. Your father's a *kulak*! See this document – it's just come in from Kamen. You made yourself scarce because your father's a *kulak*. They've been after you for two years.' I turned pale and said nothing. I hadn't been writing home for a year in case they picked up the trail. I didn't know whether the family were alive or dead and they knew no more about me. 'Where's your conscience,' he roared, and the four bars on his shoulders were shaking, 'trying to deceive the workers' and peasants' government?' I thought he was going to beat me up. He didn't though. He signed an order – gave me six hours to get out. It was November. They stripped me of my winter uniform and gave me a summer outfit, second-hand, low shoes, third-hand, a short-arsed great-coat. I was a twerp, I didn't know I could have refused to turn the stuff in and sent them to hell. And I'd got this fierce entry in my papers: 'Discharged – son of a *kulak*.' Try and get a job with that in your record! I was four days from home by train, but they wouldn't issue me with a travel warrant, or a single day's rations. They just gave me one last dinner and booted me out of the depot.

"I met my old platoon commander in the Kotlas transit prison in '38, they'd slapped a tenner on him as well, and he told me the CO and the political commissar had both been shot in '37. Proletarians or kulaks, it made no difference in '37. Or whether or not they had a conscience ... I crossed myself and said: 'So you're up there in heaven after all, Lord. You are slow to anger, but you hit hard.'"

After his two bowls of gruel Shukhov was dying for a smoke. Telling himself that he would repay it when he bought the two tumblers of home-grown from the Latvian in Hut 7, he spoke quietly to the Estonian fisherman: "Listen Eino, lend me enough for a roll-up till tomorrow. You know I won't let you down."

Eino looked Shukhov straight in the eye, then unhurriedly shifted his gaze to his so-called brother. They went halves in everything, and neither of them would lay out a shred of tobacco without asking the other. They muttered together, then Eino got out a pouch embroidered with pink thread. He took from it a pinch of factory-cut tobacco, put it on Shukhov's palm, sized it up, and added a few wisps. Just enough for one roll-up, not a scrap more.

Shukhov had newspaper of his own. He tore a bit off, rolled his cigarette, picked up a hot ember that had landed between the foreman's feet, took a long drag, another long drag, and felt a sort of dizziness all over his body, as though drink had gone to his head and his legs.

The moment he lit up green eyes glinted from the other side of the mixing room. Shukhov might have taken pity on Fetyukov and given him a drag, but he'd seen the scrounger score once that morning. Better to leave the butt for Senka Klevshin. The poor devil couldn't hear what the foreman was saying, he just sat with his head on one side looking into the fire.

Firelight fell on Tyurin's pockmarked face. He told his story without self-pity. He could have been talking about somebody else.

"I sold what odds and ends I had to a second-hand dealer for a quarter of what it was worth, I bought a couple of loaves from under the counter – bread was rationed by then. I thought I could make my way home by jumping freight trains, but they'd brought in strict laws against that as well – you could get shot trying it. And you couldn't get tickets, remember, even if you had money, and I hadn't. The streets round the station were chock-a-block with peasants in sheepskins. Some never got away, they died of hunger on the spot. All the tickets went to you know who – the OGPU, the army, people travelling on official business. You couldn't get on the platform either: there were militiamen at the doors, and security police footing it up and down the tracks on either side of the station. The sun was going down, it was cold, the puddles were icing over. Where could I spend the night? I somehow got a grip on the smooth stone wall, swung myself over with my loaves, and went into the station lavatory. I stood there a bit – nobody was after me. I walked out trying to look like a passenger, just another soldier. And there on the tracks, stood the Vladivostok-Moscow train. There was a crush round the hot-water boiler, people were passing their kettles over each other's heads. A girl in a dark blue blouse was hovering around with a two-litre kettle, afraid to get too close to the boiler. She had short little legs, and she was afraid she'd get scalded or trodden on. 'Here,' I said, 'hold my loaves and I'll get your hot water.' While I was filling up the train started moving. She was holding my loaves, crying, she didn't know what to do with them. She didn't care about the kettle. 'Run,' I said, 'run for it, I'm right behind you!' She went ahead and I followed. I caught up with her, lifted her on the train with one hand – it was tearing along by then. I hoisted myself onto the step. The conductor didn't rap my fingers or punch me in the chest. There were other soldiers in the carriage and he mistook me for one of them.''

Shukhov gave Senka a nudge, meaning finish this dog-end, poor devil. He even handed it over complete with his wooden holder – let him have a suck, it can't hurt me. Senka was a comic: he put one hand to his heart and bowed like an actor. He might be deaf but he did his best.

The foreman went on with his story.

"There were some girls, six of them, travelling in a closed compartment. Leningrad students coming back from practical work. They'd got butter and I don't know what on the table, coats dancing away on hangers, suitcases in cloth covers. They didn't know they were living – they'd had green lights all the way. We got talking and joking and drinking tea together. Which carriage are you in? they asked. I sighed and came clean: 'It's a carriage to you, it could be a hearse to me,' I told them."

It was silent in the mixing room – just the stove crackling.

"They ooh-ed and ah-ed, they had to talk it over ... But they ended up hiding me under some coats on the top bunk. The conductors had OGPU men riding with them in those days. It wasn't just your ticket they wanted – it could be your skin. The girls kept me hidden and got me as far as Novosibirsk ... Would you believe it, I had a chance later on to thank one of those girls. On Pechora. She'd caught it in the Kirov* wave in '35, she was on general duties, going down the drain fast, and I got her fixed up in the tailors' shop."

"Think we ought to make some mortar?" Pavlo asked in a whisper.

The foreman didn't hear him.

"I got to our house through the back gardens after dark. They'd whipped my father off already, and my mother and the little ones were waiting to be deported. A telegram had got there before me, and the village Soviet was on the look-out. We were in a panic, we put the light out and sat on the floor against the wall – there were activists wandering round the village looking in at

* High official whose assassination sparked a huge wave of arrests

windows. That same night I grabbed my little brother and took him off somewhere warmer, to Frunze. There was nothing to eat, for him or me. I saw some riff-raff sitting round a tar-boiler. I sat down by them and said, 'Listen, my bare-arsed friends, take my little brother as an apprentice, teach him how to live!' They took him ... I wish now I'd joined the bad lads myself."

"And you never saw your brother again?" the captain asked.

Tyurin yawned. "No, I never did." He yawned again and said, "Come on, lads, don't let it get you down! It's only a Power Station, but we'll make it a home from home. Mortar mixers – get on with it. Don't wait for the hooter."

That's the beauty of a work gang. The big bosses can't make a *zek* hurry even in working hours, but if the foreman says work during the break, work it is. Because it's the foreman who feeds you. And besides, he won't make you do it unless it's necessary.

If the mixers waited for the hooter, the bricklayers would be at a standstill.

Shukhov sighed and stood up.

"Let's go and chip ice."

He took a hatchet and a brush for the ice, his gavel, his pole, his cord and a plumb-line.

Redfaced Kildigs gave Shukhov a sour look – why jump up before the foreman? It was all right for Kildigs – he didn't have to worry where the gang's next meal was coming from: two hundred grammes of bread more or less didn't matter to the bald-headed so-and-so – he'd get by with his parcels.

He stood up all the same. He wasn't stupid. Knew he mustn't keep the whole gang waiting.

"Hold on, Vanya!" he called. "I'm with you."

You are now, chubby cheeks. If you'd been working for yourself you'd have been on your feet sooner.

(Shukhov had another reason for hurrying. They'd drawn only one plumb-line from the tool store and he wanted to get hold of it before Kildigs.)

"Just the three of them laying?" Pavlo asked the foreman. "Or shall we put another man on? There might not be enough mortar, though."

The foreman frowned and thought.

"I'll be the fourth man, Pavlo! You see to the mortar. It's a big trough, so put six men on it, some can be taking mortar out of one half, and the rest mixing some fresh in the other. I don't want any hold-ups, not so much as a minute!"

"Right then!" Pavlo sprang up. A young man, with fresh blood in his veins. The camps hadn't knocked the stuffing out of him yet. He'd got that fat face eating Ukrainian dumplings. "If you're going to lay yourself I'll make mortar. Let's see who gets most done. Where's the longest-handled shovel?"

That was the beauty of a work gang. You wouldn't expect a man like Pavlo, who'd sniped at people from the forest and raided Soviet towns at night, to break his back working in this place. But if it was for the foreman, that made all the difference.

Shukhov and Kildigs reached the top. They could hear Senka creaking up the ramp behind them. Deaf as he was he'd got the message.

The second-floor walls hadn't got very far: they were three bricks high all round, a bit higher in places. This was when the laying went best – from knee height up to your chest, without scaffolding.

There had been scaffold planks and trestles around earlier, but *zeks* had made off with the lot. Some they'd taken to other buildings, some they'd burnt, anything as long as other gangs didn't get hold of them. If they planned it right they'd have to knock some trestles together tomorrow or they'd be stuck.

You could see a long way from the top of the Power Station. The whole compound, covered with snow and deserted (the *zeks* were hiding in the warm till the hooter went). The dark towers. The sharp-pointed fence posts. The wire itself you could only see if you looked away from the sun, not into it. The sun was so bright it made you keep your eyes shut.

A little farther off you could see the power supply train. Look at all the smoke! Blackening the sky. The train started breathing hard. It always made that hoarse noise, like a man with a bad chest, before it hooted. There it was now. They hadn't got in much overtime.

Kildigs was hurrying him up.

"Hey, you, the Stakhanovite! Hurry up with that plumb-line."

Shukhov jeered back at him.

"Look at all the ice on your wall! Think you'll get it chipped off before dark? Needn't have bothered bringing your trowel."

They were in position at the walls they'd settled on before dinner, but the foreman called out to them.

"Look, lads! We'll work in twos so the mortar won't freeze in the troughs. Shukhov, you have Klevshin on your wall and I'll work with Kildigs. And Gopchik can start by clearing Kildigs' wall for me."

Shukhov and Kildigs looked at each other. Good idea. Quicker that way.

They grabbed their hatchets.

And Shukhov no longer had eyes for the distant view, the glare of the sun on snow, the labourers struggling back from their warm hiding places to finish digging holes started that morning, or strengthen the wire mesh for concrete, or put up trusses in the workshops. Shukhov saw only the wall in front of him, from the left-hand corner, where the brickwork rose in steps waist-high, to the right corner, where Kildigs' wall began. He showed Senka where to scrape off the ice, and hacked away zealously himself, using blade and haft by turns, so that ice splinters flew in all directions, sometimes hitting him in the face. He worked fast and skilfully, but without thinking about it. His mind and his eyes were studying the wall, the façade of the Power Station, two breeze-blocks thick, as it showed from under the ice. Whoever had been laying there before was either a bungler or a slacker.

Shukhov would get to know every inch of that wall as if he owned it. That dent there – it would take three courses to make the wall flush, with a thicker layer of mortar every time. That bulge couldn't be straightened out in less than two courses. He ran an invisible ruler over the wall, deciding how far he would lay from the stepped brickwork in the corner, and where Senka would start working towards Kildigs on his right. Kildigs wouldn't hold back at the corner, he decided, but would lay a few bricks for Senka to help him out. While they were tinkering in the corner Shukhov would rush more than half the wall up, so he and Senka wouldn't be left behind. He sized up how many blocks he should have ready, and where. As soon as the labourers got up top with the blocks he latched on to Alyoshka.

"Bring me mine! Put some here! And some over there!"

While Senka chipped away at the ice Shukhov took his wire brush in both hands and scoured the wall all over, working specially hard on the grooves, leaving the upper course not quite clear but with only a light film of frosted snow.

Shukhov was still scrabbling when the foreman climbed up and fixed his rod in the corner. Shukhov and Kildigs had put theirs up long ago.

Pavlo shouted from below: "Still alive up there? Mortar coming up!"

Shukhov broke out in a sweat: he hadn't put his string up yet. He decided to fix it for three courses at once, with a bit over. And to make it easier for Senka he'd take in more of the outer course and leave him a bit more inside.

While he was tightening the string over the top edge he explained to Senka with words and signs where he had to lay. The deaf man understood. Biting his lip and rolling his eyes he nodded at the foreman's corner as much as to say let's give them hell! Let's beat them to it! He laughed.

The mortar was on its way up the ramp. Four pairs would be carrying it. The foreman said not to stand troughs near the layers – the mortar would only freeze while it was being tipped into them – but to put the handbarrows down by them so they could help themselves. The carriers needn't hang around up top freezing, they could be shifting breeze-blocks closer to the layers instead. When the first two handbarrows were empty, a second lot would pass them on their way down, so there'd be no hold-ups. The first two pairs of carriers could make for the stove, defrost the lumps of mortar stuck to the handbarrows, and thaw themselves out if they had time.

The first two barrows arrived together, one for Kildigs' wall, one for Shukhov's. The mortar was barely warm, but it steamed in the frosty air. Slap it on and be quick about it or it'll freeze stiff, and you'll have to break it up with your hammer, a trowel won't budge it. And if you lay a block the least bit out of line it will freeze on lop-sided. All you can do then is knock it out with the head of your hatchet and chip the mortar away.

Shukhov didn't make mistakes, though. The blocks weren't all the same. If one of them had a corner knocked off or a kinky edge or a blister Shukhov spotted it right away and knew which way round it needed to be laid and which spot in the wall was just waiting for it.

He scooped up a trowel full of steaming mortar, slapped it on the very spot, making a note where the blocks in the row below met so that the middle of the block above would be dead centre over the groove. He slapped on just enough mortar for one block at a time. Then he grabbed a block from the pile – he was a bit careful, though, he didn't want a hole in his mittens, and those blocks were horribly scratchy. Then he smoothed the mortar down with his trowel and plopped the block on it. Then quick as quick he squared it up, tapping it into place with the side of his trowel if it wasn't sitting right, making sure it was flush with the outside of the wall and dead level widthwise and lengthwise. Because it would freeze on and stick fast right away.

Next, if any mortar had been squeezed out from under the block you had to chip if off quick and flick it away with your trowel. (In summer you could use it for the next block, but this time of year – forget it.) Then another look at the bonding in the row below – there might be a damaged block, where a bit had crumbled away, and if there was, you slapped on more mortar, thicker under the left end, and didn't just lay the block but slid it on from right to left so it squeezed out the extra mortar between itself and the block to the left. Make sure it's flush. Make sure it's flat. Block set fast. Next please!

Off to a good start. Get two courses laid and tidy up the old rough bits and it's all plain sailing. Keep your eyes skinned, now!

Shukhov was rushing the outer course to join up with Senka. And Senka, in the corner with the foreman, was letting it rip on his way towards Shukhov.

Shukhov tipped the wink to the carriers – mortar, quick, over here where I can reach it! Haven't even got time to wipe my nose!

Shukhov and Senka met up, started dipping into the same barrow and scraped the bottom.

"Mortar!" Shukhov roared over the wall.

"Coming!" Pavlo yelled back.

Fresh mortar was brought. They scooped up all the moist stuff, but the carriers would have to scrape off what had stuck to the sides. If they let a thick crust grow they were the ones who'd be lugging all that extra weight up and down. Right, you can push off! Next please!

Shukhov and the other layers had stopped feeling the cold. Once they got into their stride that first glow passed over them – the glow that makes you wet under jacket, jerkin, overshirt and undershirt. But they didn't let up for a single moment, they went on laying faster and faster, and an hour later the second glow hit them, the one that dries the sweat. The frost wasn't getting at their feet, that was the main thing, nothing else, not even that thin, nagging wind could take their minds off their work. Klevshin, though, kept knocking one foot against the other. He took size elevens, poor devil, and the boots they'd given him weren't a pair but were both too tight.

Every now and then the foreman yelled "mortar", and Shukhov echoed him.

Set a cracking pace and you become a sort of foreman

yourself. Shukhov wasn't going to fall behind the other two: to hurry the mortar up that ramp he'd have run the legs off his own brother.

After the dinner-break Buynovsky had begun by working with Fetyukov. The ramp was steep and treacherous and he didn't make a very good job of it to begin with. Once or twice Shukhov gave him a gentle touch of the whip.

"Hurry it up a bit, Captain! Captain, let's have some blocks here!"

But while the captain moved more briskly with every load, Fetyukov got lazier: the shitbag would walk along deliberately tilting the handbarrow and splashing mortar out to make it lighter.

Once Shukhov punched him in the back.

"Filthy rat! I bet you kept the men hard at it when you were the manager!"

"Foreman!" the captain shouted. "Put me with a human being! I refuse to work with this prick!"

The foreman made the switch. Fetyukov could heave blocks onto the scaffolding from below, where they could count separately how many he shifted, and Alyoshka the Baptist would work with the captain. Anybody who felt like it could order Alyoshka about, he was so meek and mild.

The captain kept egging him on. "Heave-ho me hearties! Look how fast they're laying!"

Alyoshka smiled humbly. "We can go faster if you like. Whatever you say."

They plodded off down the ramp.

A willing lad. A treasure to his mates.

The foreman shouted down to somebody. Another truck carrying breeze-blocks had just pulled up. Not a sign of one for six months, then they come in droves. Work all out while they're bringing them. There'll be hold–ups later and you'll never get back into the swing of it.

The foreman was at it again, cursing somebody down below. Something to do with the hoist. Shukhov was curious but too busy straightening out the wall. The mortar-carriers came over and told him: a mechanic had arrived to mend the engine on the hoist, and the man in charge of electrical work, a free employee, was with him. The mechanic was tinkering and the free man was watching him.

Normal, that: one working, one watching.

If they hurry up and fix the hoist we can lift the mortar and the breeze-blocks with it.

Shukhov was well on with the third row (and Kildigs had just started his third) when yet another watchdog, another bossman, oozed up the ramp – Der, the overseer of building works. A Moscovite. Supposed to have worked in a ministry.

Shukhov, close to Kildigs by now, pointed at Der.

"So what?" Kildigs said. "I never have anything to do with the bosses. Call me, though, if he falls off the ramp."

Now he'd be standing behind the layers watching. If there was one thing Shukhov couldn't endure it was these spectators. Trying to wangle himself an engineer's job, the pigfaced bastard. Started showing me how to lay bricks once. Laughed myself sick. Till you've built one house with your own hands you're no engineer. That's how I see it.

They didn't have brick buildings in Temgenyovo, the cottages were all wood-built. Even the school was a log cabin – they'd brought ten-metre tree trunks from the state forest. But when the camp suddenly needed a bricklayer – Shukhov thought he might as well be one. If you can do two things with your hands you'll soon pick up another ten.

Pity, Der tripped once but didn't fall off. Reached the top almost at a run.

"Tyu-u-rin!" he yelled, with his eyes popping out. "Tyu-rin!"

Pavlo came running up the plank behind him, still gripping his shovel.

Der's jacket was camp issue, but a nice clean, newish one. He was wearing a splendid leather cap. But it had a number on it, like everybody else's. B-731.

"What d'you want?" Tyurin went to meet him trowel in hand. His cap had slipped down over one eye.

Must be something special. Shukhov didn't want to miss it, but the mortar was getting cold in the trough. He went on laying while he listened.

"What the hell do you mean by it?" Der was yelling, spittle flying. "You're asking for more than a spell in the hole! This is a criminal offence, Tyurin! You'll get a third term!"

Shukhov suddenly caught on. He shot a glance at Kildigs. Kildigs had realised too. The tar-paper! Der had spotted the tarred paper over the window spaces.

Shukhov wasn't afraid for himself. The foreman wouldn't give him away. It was the foreman he was afraid for. Like a father to us, the foreman is. Just a pawn to them. For this sort of thing they'd just as soon fix him up with another stretch in the Arctic as not.

Shukhov had never seen the foreman look so ugly. He threw his trowel down with a clatter. Took a step towards Der. Der looked behind him – there was Pavlo, shovel in the air.

Of course! He'd brought it up on purpose.

And Senka, deaf as he was, had realised what was going on, and moved in with his hands on his hips. A tough old devil he was too.

Der blinked and looked round nervously for a bolt-hole.

The foreman put his face close to Der's. He was speaking quietly, but his voice carried up top there.

"The time's gone when a shit like you could hand out sentences. Say a single word, you bloodsucker, and your last day's come. Just you remember!"

The foreman was trembling all over. Couldn't stop trembling.

And the look on Pavlo's sharp features would cut a man in two.

Der turned pale and moved away from the ramp.

"Steady on, lads! Take it easy!" he said.

The foreman said no more, but straightened his cap, picked up his curved trowel, and went back to his wall.

Pavlo walked slowly down the plank with his shovel. Real slow.

Oh, yes. Slitting a few throats had made a difference. Just three of them – and you wouldn't know it was the same camp.

Der was afraid to stay, and afraid to go down. He stood still, hiding behind Kildigs' back.

Kildigs went on laying, like somebody weighing out medicines at the chemist's. He looked like a doctor, and he always took his time. He kept his back to Der, pretending he hadn't seen him.

Der crept over to the foreman. No bossiness about him now.

"What can I tell the site manager, Tyurin?"

The foreman went on laying and didn't look round.

"Tell him it was there already. Like that when we got here."

Der hung around a bit more. He could see they weren't about to kill him there and then. He strolled round quietly, with his hands in his pockets.

"Hey, Shcha-854," he growled. "Why are you putting the mortar on so thin?"

He had to take it out on somebody. And since nobody could find fault with Shukhov's bonding he had to say the mortar was too thin.

"With your permission," Shukhov lisped, with a bit of a grin, "if I lay it any thicker this Power Station will be letting in water all over next spring."

"You're just a bricklayer — you'd better listen to what your overseer tells you."

Der frowned and puffed out his cheeks — a habit of his.

Well, maybe it was a bit thin in places. Might have been thicker if we'd been working like human beings, not out here in the middle of winter. You ought to show a bit of consideration. We've got to earn all we can. No good trying to explain, though, if he can't see it himself.

Der went quietly down the ramp.

"You get my hoist fixed up!" the foreman shouted after him. "What d'you take us for — cart-horses? Heaving breeze-blocks up two storeys by hand!"

"You'll be paid for it!" Der answered, from halfway down — but peaceably.

"Wheelbarrow rate I suppose? Go on, get hold of a wheelbarrow and try running it up that ramp. We want handbarrow rate!"

"I wouldn't grudge you. But Accounts won't put it through at handbarrow rate."

"To hell with Accounts! I've got my whole gang carrying for four bricklayers. How much can I earn that way?"

The foreman went on laying steadily while he was shouting.

"Mor-tar!" he shouted down.

Shukhov took up the cry. "Mor-tar!" Finished levelling up the third row, now get going on the fourth. Ought really to take the string a course higher, but it'll do. We can rush up one course without it.

Der was away across the site, all hunched up. Heading for the office to get warm. Feeling a bit uncomfortable, I bet. Ought to stop and think before he takes on a wolf like the foreman. Keep on good terms with Tyurin and his like and he wouldn't have a care in the world. Nobody expects him to break his back, he gets big rations, lives in a cabin of his own – what more does he want? Wants to show how clever he is, that's what.

Somebody came up the ramp to say that the manager (electrical maintenance) and the mechanic had both left, and the hoist couldn't be mended.

So – donkey work it is.

Every job Shukhov had been on, the machinery either broke down or else the *zeks* broke it. A conveyor, say, they'd wreck by ramming a rod through the chain and putting on the pressure. Just to get a rest. If you're made to stack peeled logs all day, bent double, you can get stuck that way.

"More blocks!" the foreman shouted. He was in top gear now. The heavers and carriers got called everything under the sun.

Loud voices from below. "Pavlo says what about mortar."

"Mix some, what d'you think."

"We've still got half a trough left."

"So mix another."

It was going like a house on fire. They were on the fifth course. They'd had to do the first doubled up, but the wall was breast-high now, or nearly. Nothing to it, anyway — no windows, no doors, just two blank walls, joining up, and plenty of breeze-blocks. Should have raised the string — too late now.

"Gang 82 are handing their tools in," Gopchik reported.

The foreman flashed a look at him.

"Mind your own business, small fry, and get some blocks over here."

Shukhov looked over his shoulder. Yes, the sun was going down. A reddish sun in a sort of greyish mist. We're really getting somewhere now. Couldn't be better. On the fifth course now, so we'll just finish it off. Then level it all up.

The carriers sounded like cart-horses out of breath. The captain's grey in the face. Well, he must be forty, or getting on that way.

It was some degrees colder already. Shukhov's hands were busy, but the cold nipped his fingers through the thin mittens. And sneaked into his left boot. He stamped his foot now and then to warm it.

He could work on the wall without crouching now, but had to bend his aching back for every breeze-block and every spoonful of mortar.

"Come on, lads," he said roughly. "You could put the blocks up here on the wall for me."

The captain would have obliged, only he hadn't the strength. Wasn't used to it. But Alyoshka said:

"Right then, Ivan Denisovich, just show me where you want them."

Never says no, that Alyoshka, whatever you ask him to do. If everybody in the world was like him I'd be the same. Help anybody who asked me. Why not? They've got the right idea, that lot.

The clanging of the hammer on the rail carried across the whole site as far as the Power Station. Knocking-off time. Just when the mortar was made. That's what comes of trying too hard.

"Mortar! Let's have some mortar!" the foreman yelled.

A new batch had just been made. Nothing for it now – just keep on laying. If we don't empty the trough it'll be the devil's own job cracking it tomorrow. The mortar will be stone hard, you won't gouge it out with a pick-axe.

"Don't give up yet, boys!" Shukhov urged.

Kildigs looked angry. He didn't like rush jobs. Back home in Latvia, he said, everybody took his time and everybody was well off. But there was no getting out of it. He had to step on it, like the rest of them.

Pavlo hurried up top between the shafts of a handbarrow, bringing his trowel. He joined the bricklayers. Five trowels at work now.

Must centre blocks over the joins below. Shukhov gauged the size of the block he would need each time and shoved a gavel at Alyoshka.

"Here – square one up for me." More haste, less speed. Now that the others were out to break records Shukhov stopped forcing the pace and took a good look at the wall. He steered Senka to the left and took the right, over towards the main corner, himself. To leave a bulge in the wall or make a mess of the corner would be a disaster. Take half tomorrow to put it right.

"Hold it!" He came between Pavlo and the block he was laying and straightened it himself. Looks as if Senka's got a dent near the corner there. He darted over and straightened two blocks.

The captain hauled another load in like a willing horse. "There's another two barrow loads to come," he shouted.

On his last legs, but still pulling his weight. Shukhov's gelding, the one he had before collectivisation, had been the same. Shukhov had taken good care of him, but when strangers got their hands on him they worked him to a frazzle. And did for him in no time.

The rim of the sun had disappeared behind the earth now. Shukhov could see for himself, without Gopchik telling him, that all the other gangs had handed their tools in and men were flocking towards the guard house. (Nobody went outside the moment down tools was sounded. They weren't daft enough to stand out there freezing. They sat around in their warm corners for a bit. But at a certain moment the foreman would agree to move and the gangs streamed out all at once. They had to do it that way because convicts are such a pigheaded lot they'd be there till midnight seeing who could sit in the warm longest.)

Tyurin realised that he'd left it a bit late. The tool-maker would be calling him every name he could lay his tongue to.

"Right," he said. "No good saving shit! Hodmen – whizz down, scrape out the big trough, carry the lot to that hole over there and shovel snow on top so nobody can see it. You, Pavlo, take two men, collect the tools and hand them in. I'll send Gopchik after you with the three trowels once we've got through the last couple of barrow loads of mortar."

They jumped to it. Took Shukhov's gavel from him, untied his string. The hodmen and brick-heavers all hurried down to the mixing room – nothing left for them to do up top. Only the three bricklayers – Kildigs, Klevshin and Shukhov – stayed behind. The foreman walked round checking what they'd done. Seemed pleased.

"Good bit of bricklaying, eh? For half a day's work. Without a hoist, or any other effing thing."

Shukhov saw that Kildigs had only a bit left in his trough. But he was worried that the foreman would get a row in the tool store for keeping the trowels back. He found the answer.

"Listen, lads, you catch Gopchik up with the trowels, mine isn't counted, and I don't have to hand it in, so I can finish the job."

The foreman laughed. "They'd be mad to let you out! Any jail would be lost without you!"

Shukhov laughed back at him. And went on laying.

Kildigs carried the trowels away. Senka fed breeze-blocks to Shukhov. They tipped Kildigs' mortar into Shukhov's trough.

Gopchik ran all the way to the tool store trying to catch up with Pavlo. And Gang 104 set out across the site by itself, without its foreman. A foreman carries a lot of weight – but the convoy guards carry more. They'll make note of latecomers – and pack them off to the hole.

The crowd by the guard house had thickened alarmingly. Everybody was there by now. Looked as if the guard had turned out too to count them all again. (They count twice at every turn-out. Once with the gates shut to find out whether it's safe to open them, the second time as the men are passing through the gates. And if they fancy they see anything wrong they count yet again outside the gates.)

"To hell with the mortar," the foreman said impatiently. "Chuck it over the wall!"

"Better be off, foreman! You're more needed there!" (Shukhov generally called him Andrei Prokofievich, but working as he was now made him the foreman's equal. He didn't put it in words to himself – "I'm as good as he is" – just felt it.) "Bloody nuisance, these short working days," he called out jokingly, as the foreman strode down the ramp. "Just when you're beginning to enjoy yourself it's knocking-off time."

Only himself and the deaf man left. No good talking to him. No need anyway: he's cleverer than the lot of them, you never have to tell him anything.

Slap on the mortar! Slap on a block! Press it down a bit. Make sure it's straight. Mortar. Block. Mortar. Block.

The foreman had ordered them not to worry about wasting mortar, to chuck it over the wall and take off. But Shukhov was the sort of fool who couldn't let anything or anybody's work go to waste, and nobody would ever teach him better.

Mortar! Block! Mortar! Block!

"Enough, damn it!" Senka shouted. "Time to be off!"

He grabbed a handbarrow and was away down the ramp.

If the guards had set their dogs on him it wouldn't have stopped Shukhov. He moved quickly back from the wall to take a good look. All right. Then quickly up to the wall to look over the top from left to right. Outside straight as could be. Hands weren't past it yet. Eye as good as any spirit level.

He ran down the ramp.

Senka came running out of the mixing room and up the slope. Turned his head to shout.

"Come on!"

"Keep running. I won't be a minute."

Down into the mixing room. Can't just leave the trowel lying around. Might not be brought out tomorrow. They might pack the gang off to Sotsgorodok. Could be six months before I get back to this place. I'm not going to let that trowel get lost. Hide it, then, and hide it good and proper!

All the stoves were out in the mixing room. It was dark. He felt afraid. Not because of the dark, but because everybody had gone, he'd be the only one missing at the guard house, and the guards would pitch into him.

Still – take a good look round. He spotted a hefty stone up a corner, rolled it over, shoved the trowel behind and covered it. OK now!

Quick, catch up with Senka. He's only run a hundred yards. Wouldn't go any farther without me. Never leave anybody in the lurch, Senka wouldn't. If there's going to be trouble, we're in it together – that's Senka.

They ran side by side, the big man and the shorter man. Senka was head and shoulders taller than Shukhov, and it was a huge head he had on him.

Some people with nothing better to do run races in stadiums of their own free will. Silly devils should try running for their lives bent double after a day's work. In this cold with wet mittens and worn-out boots.

Shukhov and Senka were as hot as rabid dogs. Their own panting was all they could hear.

Still, the foreman was at the guard house, he'd explain.

They were running straight towards the crowd, and it was scary.

Hundreds of raucous voices started baying at them: cursing them up and down and calling them all the bastards in creation. Who wouldn't be scared with five hundred furious men yelling at him!

What mattered, though, was how the guards would take it.

The guards weren't bothered. The foreman was right there, in the back row. He must have explained, taken the blame on himself.

The lads went on yelling and cursing horribly. Yelling so loud that even Senka heard quite a bit; he took a deep breath and roared back. He lived his life in silence – but when he did sound off . . . ! He put up his fists, spoiling for a fight. The men stopped shouting, and some of them laughed.

"Hey, 104! Thought you said he was deaf!" They called out. "We wanted to make sure."

Everybody laughed. Guards as well.

"Form up in fives!"

They weren't opening up, though. Didn't trust themselves. They pushed the crowd back. (The idiots were all glued to the gates as though that would speed things up.)

"By-y fives! First! Second! Third!"

As they called out each five it moved forward a few metres.

While this was going on Shukhov got his breath back and looked round. Old man moon was right up there now, red and sulky-looking. Just past the full. Yesterday it had been a lot higher at that time.

Shukhov felt playful now that everything had gone so smoothly. He nudged the captain and shot a question at him.

"Here, Captain, you know science – where does it say the old moon gets to?"

"What d'you mean, where does it get to? What an

ignorant question! It's there, we just can't see it."

Shukhov wagged his head and laughed.

"So if you can't see it how d'you know it's there?"

The captain looked surprised.

"According to you, then, the moon really is new every month?"

"What's so strange about that? People are born every day, why shouldn't a moon be born every four weeks?"

The captain spat in disgust. "I never met a sailor as stupid as you. Where d'you think the old moon goes then?"

"That's what I'm asking you – where does it get to?" Shukhov showed his teeth.

"Go on, tell me."

Shukhov sighed and delivered his reply with a slight lisp.

"Where I come from they used to say God breaks up the old moon to make stars."

The captain laughed. "What savages! I never heard anything like it! So you believe in God, do you, Shukhov?"

Now Shukhov was surprised. "Of course I do. How can anybody not believe in God when it thunders?"

"Why does God do it, then?"

"Do what?"

"Break up the moon to make stars. Why, d'you think?"

"That's an easy one," Shukhov said with a shrug. "Stars fall every now and then, the holes have to be filled up."

"Turn round, blast you!" the guards were shouting. "Get lined up!"

The count had reached them. The twelfth row of five after four hundred went through with two men behind them, Buynovsky and Shukhov.

The guards were flummoxed. Consulted their tally

boards. A man short again! The rotten dogs might at least learn how to count!

They'd counted four hundred and sixty-two, and they told each other it should be four hundred and sixty-three.

The men had pressed forward to the gate again, and once again they were shoved back and it was:

"Form up in fives! First five! Second!"

The time wasted on these re-counts of theirs was not the state's, but the men's own – that's what made it all so vexatious. They still had to trudge over the steppe back to camp and queue up outside for the body search. Men from all the different sites would be racing to be searched first and dive into camp before all the others. Whichever work party arrived first was king for the day: the mess hut would be waiting, they'd have first chance to claim parcels, be first at the storeroom, first at the individual kitchen, first at the CES★ to collect letters or hand in their own to be censored, first at the sickbay, the barber's, the bath house – everywhere.

Generally the guards were in just as much of a hurry to get the men off their hands, and withdraw to their own quarters. A soldier couldn't afford to hang about, either: there was too much to do and too little time for it.

But the figures didn't add up.

As they were waving the last rows of five past, Shukhov thought for a moment that there would be three of them right at the back. But no – it was still only two.

The counters hurried over to the guard commander with their boards. There was some talk, then the commander yelled out:

"Foreman, Gang 104!"

Tyurin took half a step forward.

★Cultural and Educational Section

"Here."

"Any of yours left behind at the Power Station? Think before you answer."

"No."

"Think, or I'll tear your head off!"

"It's like I said."

But he shot a glance at Pavlo – maybe somebody had gone to sleep back there in the mixing room?"

"Form up by gangs!" the guard commander shouted. The gangs had been mixed together. When they formed fives each man had just moved up to whoever was nearest. Now there was a lot of shoving and shouting "76 – this way!" "13 – over here!" "Come on, 32!"

104 stayed where it was, behind all the rest. Shukhov was now able to see that the whole gang was empty-handed. The idiots had been working so hard they hadn't collected any kindling. Only two of them had dainty little bundles.

This was a game they played every day. Before knocking-off time the workers would collect wood-chips, sticks, bits of broken board, and carry them off tied up with a strip of rag or a bit of string. The first raid might come at the guard house. If the site manager or one of the overseers was waiting there he would order them to drop the lot. (As if by collecting wood-chips they could make up for the millions they'd sent up in smoke.) But the workers had ideas of their own. If every man in a gang got home with just a stick or two the hut would be that much warmer. Without this there was only the five kilo-grammes of coal dust issued to the hut orderlies for each stove, and you couldn't expect much warmth from that. So besides the wood they carried in their hands they broke or sawed sticks into short pieces and stuffed them under their jackets. That much they'd get past the site manager.

The guards never ordered them to drop their firewood on the work site. The guards also needed firewood, and couldn't carry it themselves. For one thing, their uniform forbade it, and for another their hands were full with the automatic weapons they needed to shoot prisoners. But when they'd marched the column up to the camp they'd give the order:

"All those from row such-and-such to row such-and-such drop your wood over here."

They weren't heartless, though: they had to leave some wood for the warders, and some for the *zeks* themselves, otherwise nothing at all would be brought in.

So the rule was that every *zek* carried some firewood every day. Sometimes you'd get it home, sometimes it would be taken from you. You never knew.

While Shukhov's eyes were combing the ground looking for chips to pick up, the foreman counted the gang and reported to the guard commander.

"104 – all present!"

Including Tsezar, who had left the other office workers and joined his own gang. There was hoar frost on his black moustache. He puffed hard at his pipe and the red glow warmed his face.

"How are things, Captain?" he asked.

Stupid question! If you're warm yourself you don't know what it's like freezing.

The captain shrugged.

"How d'you think? I've worked so hard I can hardly stand up straight."

Meaning you might at least give me a smoke.

Tsezar offered him a smoke. The captain was the only one in the gang he hobnobbed with. There was nobody else he could have a heart-to-heart talk with.

"One missing in 32!" Everybody took up the cry.

The deputy foreman of Gang 32 and another fellow peeled off to search the motor repair shops.

A buzz went through the crowd. Who was it? What was he up to?

The word reached Shukhov that it was the little dark Moldavian. Which Moldavian was that? The one they said was a Romanian spy? A real spy for once.

There were five spies in every gang, but those were made-up spies, make-believe spies. Their papers had them down as spies, but they were just ex-prisoners of war. Shukhov was one of those himself.

That Moldavian, though, was the real thing.

The guard commander took one look at his list and went black in the face. He was in for it if a spy had escaped!

The whole crowd, Shukhov as well, were furious. What sort of rotten creep, louse, shit, swine, murdering bastard was he? The sky was dark, what light there was must be coming from the moon, the frost was hardening for the night, and that mangy cur was missing! Hadn't the shit had his fill of work? Wasn't the official working day, eleven hours of it from dawn to dusk, long enough for him? Just you wait! The Prosecutor will find you some extra time!

Even Shukhov thought it weird – working and not noticing the signal.

He'd quite forgotten that he'd just been doing it himself, and had felt peeved when he saw them all crowding round the guard house too early. Now he was freezing with the rest, and fuming with the rest, and thinking that if that Moldavian kept them waiting another half hour, and the guards handed him over to the crowd they'd tear him to pieces like wolves tearing a calf!

Now the cold was really biting! Nobody could keep still – they were all stamping their feet, or taking two steps forward, two steps back.

People were wondering whether the Moldavian could be trying to escape. If he'd run off earlier in the day, that was one thing, but if he was hiding and waiting for the guards to be brought down from the watchtowers he'd wait in vain. If there were no tracks showing where he'd crawled under the wire, they'd keep the guards up there for three whole days while they searched the whole site. Or a week if need be. Any old convict knows that's what standing orders say. One way or another, the guards' life isn't worth living with somebody on the loose. They're run off their feet, can't stop to eat or sleep. Sometimes they get so furious that the runaway isn't brought back alive. They shoot him down.

Tsezar was working on the captain.

"The pince-nez dangling from the rigging for instance – remember?"

"Mm – yes." The captain was busy smoking.

"Or the baby carriage rolling and rolling down the Odessa steps?"

"Yes. But in that film life on board ship is like a puppet show."

"Maybe modern film technique makes us expect too much."

"The officers are rotters to a man."

"That's true to history!"

"So who d'you think led the men into battle? Then again, those maggots crawling on the meat look as big as earthworms. Surely there were never any maggots like that?"

"The camera can't show them any smaller!"

"I tell you what, if they brought that meat to our camp today instead of the shitty fish we get and chucked it in the pot without washing or scraping it, I think we'd ..."

Cries came from the *zeks*. "Aaaah! Ooooh!"

They'd seen three figures darting out of the auto-repair shop. Evidently the Moldavian had been found.

The crowd by the gate howled. "Oo-oo-oo-ooh."

Then when the three got closer:

"Filthy swine! Traitor! Rat! Dirty dog! Shitface! Rotten bastard!"

Shukhov joined in:

"Filthy swine!"

Well, it was no joke – he'd robbed five hundred men of more than half an hour of their time.

The Moldavian hunched his shoulders and scurried along like a mouse.

A guard shouted "Halt!" and took his number. "K-460. Where were you?" He walked up to the man as he spoke, turning his rifle butt end forward.

There were shouts from the crowd of "Bastard!" "Dog's vomit!" "Rotten shit!"

But others quietened down as soon as the sergeant turned his rifle round.

The Moldavian said nothing, just lowered his head and backed away from the sergeant. The deputy foreman of Gang 32 stepped forward.

"The rotten bastard climbed up on the plasterers' scaffolding to hide from me, managed to get warm up there and fell asleep."

He gave the man a kidney punch. And a rabbit punch.

That way he sent him staggering out of the sergeant's reach.

But as the man reeled back a Hungarian belonging to

the same gang, 32, sprang forward, kicked his behind, and kicked it again. (Hungarians don't like Romanians at the best of times.)

A bit different from spying, eh? Any idiot can be a spy. Spies live in comfort, spies have fun. You won't find a tenner on general duties in a hard-labour camp quite so easy.

The sergeant lowered his rifle,. and the guard commander yelled:

"Get away from the gates! Form up in fives!"

Counting again, the bastards! Why now, when they'd cleared it all up? An ugly noise went through the ranks. All the hatred they'd felt for the Moldavian was switched to the guards. They kept up their din and made no effort to move away from the gates.

"What's this, then?" the guard commander bellowed. "Want me to sit you down on the snow? Don't think I won't. I'll keep you here till morning!"

He would, too. Nothing out of the ordinary. Prisoners had been made to sit down often enough before. Or even lie down. "Lie down! Guards – guns at the ready!"

The *zeks* knew this sort of thing could happen. They started inching back from the gates. The guards encouraged them with shouts of "Get back! Get back there!"

Zeks in the rear shouted angrily at those in front. "What are you leaning on the gate for anyway, silly creeps?" The mob was slowly forced backwards.

"Form up in fives! First five! Second! Third!"

By now the moon was shining full strength. The redness had gone and it had brightened up. It was a good quarter of the way up. The evening had gone to waste. Damn that Moldavian. Damn the guards. Damn this life of ours.

The front ranks, once counted, turned and stood tiptoe trying to see whether there'd be two men or three left in the rear. That was now a matter of life and death.

Shukhov thought for a moment there were going to be four. He felt weak with fright. One too many! Another re-count! But it turned out that Fetyukov, the scavenger, had gone to beg the captain's dog-end, and hadn't got back to his place in time, so it looked as though there was one man extra.

The deputy guard commander lost his temper and punched Fetyukov in the neck.

Serve him right!

Now there were three in the rear rank. Got it right at last. Thank God for that!

"Get away from the gates!" The guards forced them back again.

This time the *zeks* didn't grumble. They could see soldiers coming out of the guard house and cordoning off a space on the other side of the gate.

Which meant that they would be allowed through.

The free overseers were nowhere to be seen, nor the site manager. The lads would be getting their wood out.

The gates were flung wide. The guard commander and a checker were waiting once again by a log railing just outside.

"First five! Second! Third!"

If the numbers tallied this time the sentries would be taken off the towers. They had quite a long way to trudge round the boundary fence from the farthest towers. Only when the last *zek* was led out of the compound and the count came out right would the towers get a telephone call telling the guards to come down. Not a minute before. If the guard commander had any sense he'd move out right away! He knew the *zeks* couldn't run for it, and he knew the men from the towers would catch up with the column. But a dimwitted commander might be afraid he wouldn't have men enough to handle the *zeks*, so he'd wait around.

Today's commander was one of those fatheads. He decided to wait.

The *zeks* had been out in the cold all day, almost frozen to death. And now they'd been standing freezing for a whole hour since knocking-off time. What really got them down, though, was not the cold but the maddening thought that their evening was ruined. There'd be no time for anything back in camp.

"How do you come to know so much about life in the British navy?" somebody in the next rank was asking.

"Well, it's like this, I spent nearly a month on a British cruiser, had my own cabin. I was liaison officer with one of their convoys."

"That explains everything. Quite enough for them to pin twenty-five on you."

"Sorry, I don't go along with all that destructive liberal criticism. I think better of our legal system."

Bullshit, Shukhov said. (To himself – he didn't want to get involved.) Senka Klevshin was with the Americans for two days and he got lumbered with twenty-five. You were sitting pretty on that ship of theirs for a month – how long does that entitle you to?

"Only after the war the British admiral took it into his blasted head to send me a souvenir, a token of gratitude, he called it. What a nasty surprise, and how I cursed him for it!"

It was queer when you came to think of it. The bare steppe, the deserted site, the snow sparkling in the moonlight. The guards spaced out ten paces from each other, guns at the ready. The black herd of *zeks*. One of them, in the same sort of jacket as the rest, Shch-311, had never known life without golden epaulettes, had palled up with a British admiral, and here he was toting a handbarrow with Fetyukov.

You can turn a man upside down, inside out, any way you like.

The guards were all there now, and it was "Quick march! Speed it up!" Just like that. No "prayers" this time.

Speed it up? The hell we will. No good hurrying now all the other work parties have gone on ahead. Without a word spoken the *zeks* all had the same idea: you've held us up, now we'll hold you up. We know you're just as keen as we are to get in the warm.

"Step on it!" the guard commander shouted. "Front marker – step on it!"

Like hell we will!

The *zeks* plodded on, heads down, like men going to a funeral. Nothing to lose now, we're last back in camp anyway. You wouldn't treat us like human beings, so bust a gut shouting.

The shouts – "Step on it!" – went on for a while, till the guard commander realised that the *zeks* wouldn't go any faster. Shooting was out of the question: they were walking in column, in ranks of five, in good order. There was nothing the guard commander could do to make them move more quickly. (In the morning the *zeks*' only hope of salvation is ambling to work slowly. Move briskly and you'll never finish your time – you'll run out of steam and collapse.)

They went on steadily, holding themselves back. Crunching through the snow. Some chatting quietly, some not bothering. Shukhov was trying to remember

what he'd left undone in camp that morning. Oh, yes –
the sickbay! Funny, that – he'd forgotten all about it while
he was working.

They'd be seeing patients in the sickbay right now. He
might still be in time if he skipped supper. But he didn't
have much of an ache any more. They wouldn't even take
his temperature. Just a waste of time. He'd got by without
doctors so far. And that lot could doctor you right into
your coffin. Supper, not the sickbay, was more attractive
right now. How to manage a bit extra? The only hope was
that Tsezar would get a parcel, it was high time he did.

A change suddenly came over the column of *zeks*. It
wavered, stumbled, shuddered, muttered, and all at once
the fives at the rear, Shukhov among them, were running
to keep pace with those in front. They would walk a few
paces – and start running again. When the tail-end reached
the hilltop Shukhov saw to their right, some distance
away on the steppe, another black column on the move.
The others must have spotted this column and speeded up
to cut across its path.

It could only be the party from the engineering works –
three hundred men. They too must have been unlucky
enough to be kept behind. Shukhov wondered why.
Sometimes they were kept back for work reasons – to
finish repairing some machine or other. Didn't matter a
lot to them, they were in the warm all day.

Now it was devil take the hindmost. The lads were
running, really running. The guards too broke into a trot,
with the guard commander shouting:

"Don't get strung out too far! Close up at the back
there! Close up!"

Stop your yelping, God damn it! We *are* closing up,
what d'you think we're doing?

Whatever they'd been talking or thinking about was forgotten. The whole column had one thing and one thing only on its mind.

"Catch them up! Beat them to it!"

Things were all mixed up. No more sweet or sour. No more guard or *zek*. Guards and *zeks* were friends. The other column were the enemy.

Their spirits rose. Their anger vanished.

"Hurry it up! Get a move on!" the rear ranks shouted to those ahead.

Shukhov's column burst into the settlement and lost sight of the engineers beyond the houses. Now they were racing blind. Shukhov's column had a better footing, in the middle of the road. And the guards at the sides of the street stumbled less. Now, if ever, was the time to squeeze the others out!

There was another good reason for getting in front of the engineers – it took longer to search them at the guard houses. Since throat-cutting had broken out in the camp the bosses reckoned that the knives must be made at the engineering works and smuggled in. So the engineers were frisked with extra care as they entered the camp. In late autumn, with the ground already chilly, the shout would go up:

"Shoes off, engineers! Hold your shoes in your hands!" And they were frisked barefoot.

Even now, frost or no frost, the guards would pick on somebody at random – "You there, off with your right boot! You over there – left one off!"

The *zek* would simply have to hop on the other foot while one boot was turned upside down and the footrag shaken to make sure there was no knife.

Shukhov had heard – he didn't know whether it was true or not – that the engineers had brought two volleyball posts into the camp that summer, with all the knives hidden inside them. Ten big knives in each. One or two had been found lying around.

Half-running, they passed the new recreation centre, the free workers' houses, the woodworking plant, and pushed on to the turn towards the guard house.

"Hoo-oo-oo-oo-oo!" the column cried with a single voice.

That road junction was their goal. The engineers, a hundred and fifty metres to the right, had fallen behind.

They could take it easy now. The whole column rejoiced. Like rabbits finding that frogs, say, are afraid even of them.

And there it was – the camp. Just as they had left it. Darkness, lights over the tight fence round the compound, a dense battery of lamps blazing in front of the guard house, the search area flooded with what could have been sunlight.

But before they reached the guard house the guard commander shouted "Halt!"

He handed his sub-machine gun to a soldier and ran over to the column (they're told not to get too close gun in hand).

"Those on the right carrying wood – drop it on the right!"

Those on the outside, where he could see them, didn't try to hide their wood. One bundle flew through the air, a second, a third. Some tried to hide their wood inside the column but their neighbours turned on them.

"You'll make them take everybody else's! Chuck it down like a good boy!"

Who is the convict's worst enemy? Another convict. If *zeks* didn't squabble among themselves the bosses would have no power over them.

"Quick – ma-arch!" the second-in-command shouted.
And they made for the guard house.

Five roads met at the guard house and an hour earlier
they had all been crowded with prisoners from other
work sites. If some day those roads became streets lined
with buildings the future civic centre would surely be
where the guard house and the frisking area now were.
And where work parties now pressed in from all sides,
parades would converge on public holidays.

The warders were there waiting, warming themselves
in the guard house. They came out and took their stand
across the roadway.

"Undo your jackets! Undo your jerkins!" Warders'
arms wide open. Ready to embrace – and frisk. Ready to
slap each man's sides. Same as in the morning, more or
less.

Unbuttoning wasn't too terrible now they were nearly
home.

Yes – that's what they all called it, "Home".

Their days were too full to remember any other home.

After they'd frisked the head of the column Shukhov
went up to Tsezar and said: "Tsezar Markovich! When we
get past the guard house I'll run and queue at the parcel
room."

Tsezar turned his heavy black moustache (white now at
the bottom) in Shukhov's direction.

"What's the point, Ivan Denisovich? There may not be
a parcel."

"So what have I got to lose? I'll wait ten minutes and if
you don't come I'll get back to the hut." (Thinking to
himself if Tsezar doesn't come somebody else may, and I
can sell him my place in the queue.)

But it looked like Tsezar wanted that parcel pretty
badly.

"All right, then," he said, "run and get a place, Ivan Denisovich. But don't stay more than ten minutes."

The search was getting closer. Shukhov moved along without fear. He had nothing to hide this time. He took his time unbuttoning his jacket, and loosened the canvas belt round his jerkin.

He hadn't remembered having anything forbidden, but wariness had become second nature after eight years inside. So he plunged his hand into the sewn-on pocket to make sure that it was empty – though he knew very well that it was.

Ah, but there was the little bit of broken blade! The one he'd picked up at the work site that morning, not wanting to see it wasted, but hadn't meant to bring into the camp.

He hadn't meant to – but now that he had brought it, it would be a terrible pity to throw the thing away. You could hone it into a nice little knife – shoemaker's or tailor's type, whichever you wanted.

If he'd thought of carrying it in he'd also have thought up some good way of hiding it. There were only two ranks in front of him – and now the first of those peeled off and went to be frisked. He had to decide quick as a flash whether to use the cover of the rank in front and drop the blade on the snow while nobody was looking (it would be found afterwards, but they wouldn't know whose it was), or to keep it.

That bit of steel could cost him ten days in the hole if they decided it was a knife.

But a cobbler's knife was an earner, it meant extra bread!

Pity to throw it away.

Shukhov slipped it into his padded mitten.

The next five were ordered to step forward for frisking.

That left the last three men in the full glare of the lights:

Senka, Shukhov and the fellow from Gang 32 who had run after the Moldavian. Just the three of them, and five warders stood facing them. So Shukhov could play it smart and choose which of the two warders on the right to approach. He ignored the young one with a high flush and chose the older man with a grey moustache. He was more experienced, of course, and could easily have found the blade if he had wanted to, but at his age he must hate the job like poison.

He'd taken off both mittens and was clutching them in one hand with the empty one sticking out. He grasped the rope girdle in the same hand, unbuttoned his jerkin completely, obligingly plucked up the skirts of jacket and jerkin (he had never been so forthcoming at the search-point before, but he wanted to show that he had nothing to hide) and at the command went up to grey whiskers.

The grey one patted Shukhov's sides and back, tapped the sewn-on pocket from outside – nothing there – fingered the skirts of the jerkin and jacket, gave a farewell squeeze to the mitten Shukhov was holding out, and found it empty ...

When the warder squeezed his mitten Shukhov felt as if somebody had his guts between pincers. A squeeze like that on the other mitten, and he'd be done for – into the hole, on three hundred grammes a day, no hot food for two days at a time. He imagined himself getting weaker and weaker from hunger, and thought how hard it would be to get back to his present wiry (not too well fed, but not starving) condition.

And he offered up a silent agonised prayer: "Save me, Lord! Don't let them put me in the hole!"

All these thoughts passed through his head while the warder was feeling the first mitten and letting his hand stray to the one behind it (he would have felt both at once, if Shukhov had held one in each hand). But at that very moment they heard the warder in charge of the search, in a hurry to get off duty, call out to the guards:

"Bring up the engineers!"

So the grey-moustached warder, instead of tackling Shukhov's other mitten, waved him through. Scot free.

Shukhov ran to catch up with his team-mates. They were already drawn up in fives between the two long log-rails that looked like the hitching place at a country market, and formed a sort of paddock for the column. He ran lightly, no longer feeling the ground under his feet, forgetting to say another prayer, of gratitude this time, because he was in too much of a hurry, and anyway there was no point in it now.

The guards who had marched Shukhov's column in had now all moved over to make way for the engineers' guards and were only awaiting their commander. The wood dropped by the column before the frisk had been collected by the guards, and that confiscated by the warders during the search had been piled up by the guard house.

The moon was sailing higher and higher and the frost was tightening its grip in the bright snowy night.

The guard commander, who had gone to the guard house to recover his receipt for four hundred and sixty-three head, had a word with Pryakha, Volkovoy's second-in-command, who called out "K-460".

The Moldavian, who had buried himself in the depths of the column, heaved a sigh and went over to the right-hand hitching rail. He kept his head down and his shoulders hunched.

"Over here!" Pryakha's finger showed him the way round the hitching rail.

The Moldavian went. He was ordered to put his hands

behind his back and stand still.

So they meant to pin a charge of attempted escape on him. He'd be slung in the camp jail.

Two sentries took their stand to right and left behind the paddock and just short of the gates. The gates, three times the height of a man, opened slowly, and the order rang out:

"Form up in fives!" (No need for "get away from the gates" this time: camp gates always open inwards, so that if the *zeks* should mob them from inside they can't unhinge them.)

"Number One! Two! Three!"

Standing there to be counted through the gate of an evening, back in camp after a whole day of buffeting wind, freezing cold, and an empty belly, the *zek* longs for his ladleful of scalding hot watery evening soup as for rain in time of drought. He could knock it back in a single gulp. For the moment that ladleful means more to him than freedom, more than his whole past life, more than whatever life is left to him.

The *zeks* go in through the camp gates like warriors returning from a campaign – blustering, clattering, swaggering – "make way there, can't you!"

The trusty looking at the wave of returning *zeks* through the staff hut window feels afraid.

After the evening count, the *zek* is a free man again for the first time since roll-call at 6.30 in the morning. Through the great camp gates, through the smaller gates to the inner compound, along the midway between another pair of "hitching rails" – and every man could go his own way.

But not the foremen. A work-assigner rounds them up with shouts of "Foremen! To the PPS!"

To try on tomorrow's horse collar.

Shukhov hurtled past the jail house, between the huts and into the parcel room. While Tsezar, preserving his dignity, walked at a leisurely pace in the other direction, to where there was already a buzzing swarm of *zeks* round a plywood board nailed to a post and bearing the names written in indelible pencil of those who had parcels waiting for them.

They generally write on plywood, not paper, in the camps. It's tougher and more reliable. The screws and the work-assigners jot down their head counts on plywood. You can scrape the figures off next day and use it again. Quite economical.

Another chance here for those left behind in camp to toady: they read on the board the name of a man who's got a parcel, meet him out on the midway and tell him the number. It's not worth a lot – but even that may earn you the odd cigarette.

Shukhov ran to the parcel room – a lean-to built onto one of the huts, with a lobby tacked onto it. The lobby had no outer door, and the cold was free to enter – but it was still somehow cosier than outside. At least it had a roof.

The queue was all round the lobby wall. Shukhov got in line. There were at least fifteen in front of him. More than an hour's wait, which would take him exactly to lights out. Those from the Power-Station column who'd gone to look at the list would be behind him. So would the engineers. They might have to come back first thing in the morning.

Men in the queue had bags and sacks. On the other side of the door (Shukhov had heard said – he had never himself received a parcel in this camp) they opened the regulation boxes with a hatchet and a warder took every article out with his own hands, cutting it up, breaking it in two, prodding it or pouring it out to examine it. Jars or cans containing liquid would be broached and emptied – all you'd get was what you caught in your hands or netted in a towel. For some reason they were afraid to hand over the containers. If there was any sort of pie or cake, any unusual sweet, any sausage or smoked fish, the warder would take a bite. (Start demanding your rights and he'd give you the treatment – this is forbidden, that isn't allowed – and you'd end up with nothing. Whoever gets a parcel has to give and keep on giving – the warder's only the beginning.) When they've finished searching they still won't give you the box it came in – just sweep the lot into a bag, or the skirts of your jacket and clear off. Next, please. They can hurry a man up so much he leaves something on the counter. He needn't bother going back. It won't be there.

Shukhov had received a couple of parcels back in Ust-Izhma, but he'd written to his wife not to send any more, not to rob the kids, it only went to waste.

It had been easier for Shukhov to feed his whole family as a free man than it was to feed just himself in the camps, but he knew what those parcels cost, and you couldn't go on milking your family for ten years on end. Better to do without.

That's what he'd decided, but whenever anybody in the gang or the hut got a parcel (somebody did almost every day) he felt a pang – why isn't it for me? And although he had strictly forbidden his wife to send anything even at Easter, and never went to look at the list on the post – except for some rich workmate – he sometimes found himself expecting somebody to come running and say:

"Why don't you go and get it, Shukhov? There's a parcel for you."

Nobody came running.

As time went by he had less and less to remind him of the village of Temgenyovo and his cottage home. Life in camp kept him on the go from getting-up time to lights out. No time for brooding on the past.

Standing among men who were savouring already the fatback they'd shortly sink their teeth into, the butter they'd smear on their bread, the sugar they'd sweeten their tea with, Shukhov's mind ran on one single desire – that he and his gang would get into the mess hut in time to eat their skilly hot. Cold it wasn't worth half as much.

He reckoned that if Tsezar hadn't found his name on the list he'd have been back in the hut washing himself long ago. If his name was there, he'd be collecting sacks, plastic mugs and wrapping paper. That was why Shukhov had promised to wait ten minutes.

Standing in the queue he heard a piece of news. No Sunday off this week, they were being diddled out of Sunday again. Just what he, and everybody else, had expected. If there were five Sundays in a month they were allowed three and hustled off to work on the other two. He'd expected it all right, but hearing it still gave him a nasty turn. Who wouldn't grieve for his precious Sunday rest? Of course, what they were saying in the queue was true enough: your day off could be hell even in camp, they could always think up something for you to do, build a bit on to the bath house, or wall up a passage between huts, or tidy up the yard. Then there was changing mattresses, shaking them, and squashing the bugs in the bunks. Or else they could take it into their heads to check the description in your dossier. Or else there was stock-taking: get all your belongings out in the yard and sit there half the day.

Nothing seemed to upset them more than a *zek* sleeping after breakfast.

The queue moved forward, slowly but steadily. Some people went inside, out of turn, shoving past the man at the head of the queue without a by-your-leave. The barber for one, and a book-keeper, and a man from the CES. These weren't common or garden *zeks* but well-fixed trusties, the lousiest bastards of the lot, who spent all their time in camp. The working *zeks* regarded these people as utter shits (and *they* thought the same of the *zeks*). But it was useless picking a quarrel with them: the trusties were all in cahoots with each other, and with the warders too.

Anyway, there were still ten men in front of Shukhov, and another seven had fallen in behind, when Tsezar, wearing the new fur hat somebody had sent him from outside, came in through the opening, ducking his head. (Really something, that hat. Tsezar had greased somebody's palm, and got permission to wear it – a neat new town hat. Other people had even their shabby old army caps snatched from them, and were given ratty camp-issue caps instead.)

Tsezar smiled at Shukhov and got talking to a queer old bird in glasses who'd been reading a newspaper all the time he was in the queue.

"Aha! Pyotr Mikhailich!"

They opened up for each other like poppies in bloom.

"Look, I've got a recent *Evening Moscow*. Sent in a wrapper," the queer fellow said.

"Have you now!" Tsezar stuck his nose into the same paper. The bulb hanging from the ceiling was as dim as dim – how could they make anything out in that small print?

"There's a most interesting review of Zavadsky's premiere!"

These Moscovites would scent each other a long way

off, like dogs. And when they got together they had their
own way of sniffing each other all over. And they gabbled
ever so fast, seeing who could get most words in. And
when they were at it there'd only be the odd Russian
word – it was like listening to Latvians or Romanians.

Anyway, Tsezar had all his bags ready.

"So, I'll er ... be off now, Tsezar Markovich," Shukhov lisped.

Tsezar raised his black moustache from the newspaper.

"Of course, of course. Let's see, now, who's ahead of
me? Who's behind me?"

Shukhov carefully explained who was where, and
without waiting for Tsezar to mention it asked:

"Shall I fetch your supper for you?" (Meaning bring it
in a mess tin from the mess hall to the hut. It was strictly
forbidden, and any number of orders had been issued on
the subject. If you were caught the mess tin was emptied
onto the ground and you were put in the hole – but people
went on doing it, and always would, because a man with
jobs to do would never get to the mess hut on time with
his own gang.)

Shukhov's real thought was "You'll let me have your
supper, won't you? You wouldn't be that stingy! You
know there's no gruel at supper-time, just skilly without
trimmings."

Tsezar gave him a little smile. "No, no, eat it yourself,
Ivan Denisovich."

That was all he was waiting for. He fluttered out of the
ante-room like an uncaged bird and was off across the
compound as fast as he could go.

Zeks were dashing around all over the place! At one
time the camp commandant had given orders that *zeks*
were not to walk about the camp singly. Whenever
possible they should be marched in gangs. And where it

was quite impossible for a whole gang to go together – to the sickbay, say, or the latrine – a group of four or five should be made up and one man put in charge to march them there, wait, and march them back again.

The commandant set great store by that order. Nobody dared argue with him. The warders grabbed lone wanderers, took their numbers, hauled them off to the jail house – but in the end the order was ditched. Quietly – as so many loud-mouthed orders are. Suppose they themselves wanted to call somebody in to see the godfather – they weren't going to send an escort party with him! Or suppose one man wanted to collect his food supply from the storeroom – why should another man have to go with him? Or say somebody took it into his head to go and read the papers in the CES – who on earth would want to go with *him*? One man has to take his boots to be mended, another is off to the drying room, somebody else just wants to wander from hut to hut (that's more strictly forbidden than anything else!) – how are you going to stop them?

The fat pig was trying to deprive the *zek* of the last scrap of liberty remaining to him. But it didn't work.

Meeting a warder on the way, and raising his cap to him just to be on the safe side, Shukhov ran into the hut. Inside there was uproar: somebody's rations had been rustled during the day. Men were shouting at the orderlies, and they were shouting back. But 104's corner was empty.

Shukhov's idea of a happy evening was when they got back to the hut and didn't find the mattresses turned upside down after a daytime search.

He rushed to his bedplace, shrugging off his jacket on the way. Up went his jacket, up went the mittens with the bit of metal in one of them, deep into the mattress went his fumbling hand – and his bread was still where he had put it that morning! Lucky he'd sewn it in! Outside at a trot! To the mess hut!

He dashed to the mess without bumping into a warder. Only *zeks* wandered across his path, arguing about rations.

Outside under the bright moon it was getting lighter all the time. All the lamps were dim, and the huts cast black shadows. The entrance to the mess hut was up four steps and across a wide porch, also now in the shadows. But a little lamp swayed above it, squeaking in the cold. Frost, or dirt, gave every lightbulb a rainbow-coloured halo.

Another of the commandant's strict orders was that the gangs should go in two at a time. On reaching the mess, the order went on to say, gangs should not mount the steps but re-form in ranks of five and stand still until the mess orderly let them in.

Limpy had hooked the mess orderly's job and held on to it for dear life. He'd promoted his limp to a disability but the bastard was fighting fit. He'd found himself a birch thumb-stick and stood on the porch using it to pin back anybody who started up the steps before he gave the order. Well, not everybody. Limpy had a quick eye and knew who was who even in the shadows and from the rear. He wasn't going to strike anybody who might give him a smack in the kisser. He only beat those who'd been beaten into shape for him. He'd nailed Shukhov once.

"Orderly" he was called. But when you thought of it he was a prince. The cooks were his pals!

This time, whether because the gangs had all rolled up at once, or because it had taken so long to get things sorted out, a dense crowd swarmed around the porch, with

Limpy, his stooge and the mess manager up above. The sons of bitches could do without warders.

The mess manager was an overstuffed swine with a head like a pumpkin and shoulders a yard and a half across. He was so strong he looked fit to burst, and walked in jerks as though his legs and arms had springs instead of joints. He wore a white fur hat, without a number patch – not one of the free workers had a hat like that. He wore also an Astrakhan waistcoat, with a little number patch no bigger than a postage stamp on his chest – to humour Volkovoy. There wasn't even a patch of that size on his back. The mess manager bowed to nobody, and the *zeks* were all afraid of him. He held thousands of lives in one hand! He nearly got beaten up once but the cooks all rushed to the rescue – and what a bunch of thugs they were!

It would be a disaster if 104 had gone through already. Limpy knew the whole camp by sight and with the mess manager there he wouldn't let you past with the wrong gang. He'd be looking for somebody to make a monkey of. Prisoners sometimes sneaked over the porch rails behind Limpy's back. Shukhov had done it himself. But, with the manager there, you couldn't do it – he'd bounce you so hard you'd just about make it to the sickbay.

Quick now, up to the porch and try and find out in the dark whether 104 are among that mass of identical black coats.

Just then the gangs began heaving and shoving (nothing else for it – lights out soon!), as though they were storming a fortress, taking the steps one at a time and swarming onto the porch.

"Halt, you sons of bitches!" Limpy roared, raising his stick at those in front. "I'll split somebody's head open in a minute!"

"We can't help it!" those in front yelled in reply. "They're shoving from behind."

The shoving was coming from behind all right, but the front rows were hoping to go flying through the mess-hut door and didn't put up much resistance.

Limpy held his staff across his chest like the barrier at a level crossing and charged the front rank full tilt. His stooge also gripped the staff, and even the mess manager wasn't too proud to soil his hands on it. They were pushing downhill, and they were stronger – they got meat to eat – so the *zeks* gave ground. The front rank reeled back down the steps onto those behind them and they in turn onto those still further back, toppling them over like sheaves.

Some of the crowd yelled "Fuck you, Limpy, you bastard," but they took care not to be spotted. The rest collapsed in silence, and rose in silence, quick as they could, before they were trampled.

The steps were cleared. The mess manager withdrew along the porch, and Limpy stood on the top step laying down the law:

"Sort yourselves out in fives, you blockheads, how many more times do I have to tell you? I'll let you in when I'm good and ready!"

Shukhov was so happy it hurt when he spotted what looked like Senka Klevshin's head right up by the porch. He set his elbows to work as fast as they'd go, but there was no breaking through that solid wall of backs.

"Gang 27!" Limpy shouted. "In you go!"

Gang 27 hopped onto the porch and rushed for the door. The rest surged up the steps in their wake, pushed from behind. Shukhov was one of those shoving with all his might. The porch shook and the lamp above it was squeaking.

Limpy flared up. "At it again, you scum?" His stick played on backs and shoulders and men were knocked flying into those behind. The steps were clear again.

From down below Shukhov saw Pavlo up beside Limpy. Pavlo always led the gang to the mess, Tyurin wouldn't rub shoulders with a mob like this.

"One-o-four, form up in fives," Pavlo shouted down at them. "And you make way there, friends!"

The friends would be hanged first.

Shukhov shook the man in front.

"You with your back to me, let me through! That's my gang."

The man would have been glad to let him through, but was wedged in himself. The crowd swayed, risking suffocation for the sake of its skilly, its lawful entitlement of skilly.

Shukhov tried something else: he grabbed the rails to his left, shifted his hold to the post supporting the porch and took off from the ground. His feet bumped against somebody's knees, he collected a few punches in the ribs and a few foul names, but then he was in the clear: standing on the top step with one foot on the porch. His team-mates spotted him and reached out to help him.

The mess manager, leaving the porch, looked round from the door.

"Two more gangs, Limpy."

"One-o-four!" Limpy shouted. "Where d'you think you're going, scum?" He brought his staff down on an intruder's neck.

"One-o-four!" Pavlo shouted, letting his men through.

"Phew!" Shukhov burst into the mess. And was off looking for empty trays without waiting for Pavlo to tell him.

The mess was its usual self – frosty air steaming in from the door, men at the tables packed as tight as seeds in a sunflower, men wandering between tables, men trying to barge their way through with full trays. But Shukhov was used to all this after so many years, and his sharp eye saw something else: Shch-208 was carrying only five bowls, so that must be his gang's last tray, otherwise it would be a full one.

Shukhov, behind him, slipped the words into his ear: "I'll come and get the tray, pal – I'm right behind you."

"That chap over by the window's waiting for it, I promised him..."

"He can take a running jump – should've kept his eyes open."

They made a deal.

Shch-208 carried his tray to the table and unloaded it. When Shukhov grabbed it, the other man, the one who'd been promised, rushed over and started tugging at the other side. He was a weakling compared with Shukhov, though. Shukhov pushed the tray at him as he pulled, he reeled back against a roof support, and the tray was wrenched from his hands. Shukhov tucked it under his arm and trotted off to the serving hatch.

Pavlo, standing in line there, dismally waiting for trays, was overjoyed to see him.

"Ivan Denisovich!" He pushed past the deputy foreman of Gang 27. "Let me through! No good you standing there! I've got trays!"

Sure enough, Gopchik, the little scamp, was lugging another one over.

"They took their eyes off it so I nicked it," he said with a laugh.

Gopchik had the makings of a really good campdweller. Give him another three years, let him grow up a bit, and fate had something good in store for him – a bread-cutter's job at least.

Pavlo ordered Yermolaev, the tough Siberian (another ex-POW doing ten), to take the second tray and sent Gopchik to look for a table where supper was nearly over. Shukhov rested one corner of his tray on the counter and waited.

"One-o-four!" Pavlo announced through the hatch.

There were five hatches altogether: three to serve ordinary prisoners, one for those on special diet (a dozen with stomach ulcers, and all the book-keepers for a kickback) and one for the return of dirty bowls (with people round it fighting to lick them). The counters were not much more than waist-high. The cooks couldn't be seen through the hatches, only their hands and ladles.

This cook's hands were white and well-manicured, but strong and hairy. A boxer's hands, not a cook's. He took a pencil and ticked off something on a list pinned up behind the partition.

"One-o-four – twenty-four."

So Panteleyev had crawled over to the mess. Not ill at all, the son of a bitch.

The cook picked up a huge ladle, a three-litre one, and stirred the pail busily. (It had just been refilled, almost to the top, and steam billowed out of it.) Then he grabbed a smaller, seven-hundred-and-fifty-gramme ladle, and began dishing out the skilly, without dipping very deep.

"One, two, three, four..."

Shukhov took note which dishes had been filled before the solids had sunk to the bottom of the pail, and which held thin stuff, nothing but water. He lined up ten bowls on his tray and carried it off. Gopchik was waving to him from near the second row of pillars.

"Over here, Ivan Denisovich, over here!"

Carrying a tray laden with bowls is not as easy as it looks. Shukhov glided along, taking care not to jolt the tray, and leaving the hard work to his vocal cords.

"Hey, you, Kh-920! Look out, old fellow! ... Out of the way there, laddie!"

In a crush like that it's a tricky business carrying just one bowl to the table without spilling it, and Shukhov had ten of them. All the same there were no fresh splashes on the tray when he set it down gently on the end of the table liberated by Gopchik. He even skilfully turned the tray so that he would be sitting at the corner with the two bowls of really thick skilly.

Yermolaev arrived with another ten bowls, and Gopchik and Pavlo hurried over with the last four in their hands. Kildigs came next, with some bread on a tray. Food today was according to amount of work done – some had earned two hundred grammes, some three hundred, and Shukhov four hundred. He took his four hundred – a big crust – and two hundred grammes from the middle of the loaf, which was Tsezar's ration.

The gang trickled in from all over the mess to take their supper away and lap it up wherever they could sit. Shukhov handed out the bowls, ticking off each man as he collected, and keeping an eye on his own corner of the tray. He had slipped his spoon into one of the bowls of thick skilly to show that it was taken. Fetyukov was one of the first to pick up a bowl. He carried it off, realising that there would be slim pickings in his own gang today and that he might have more luck scavenging around the mess. Somebody might leave a spot. (Whenever a man pushed his bowl away without emptying it others swooped like birds of prey, sometimes several at once.)

Shukhov and Pavlo totted up the portions. It looked

about right. Shukhov slipped Pavlo a bowl of the thick stuff for Andrei Prokofievich, and Pavlo poured it into a narrow German flask with a lid. He could carry it out hugged to his chest under his coat.

They surrendered their trays. Pavlo sat down to his double portion, and Shukhov to his two bowls. No more talk. The sacred minutes had arrived.

Shukhov took off his cap and put it on his knees. He checked one bowl, then the other, with his spoon. Not too bad, there was even a bit of fish. The skilly was always a lot thinner in the evening than in the morning: a *zek* had to be fed in the morning so that he could work, but in the evening he'd sleep, hungry or not, and wouldn't peg out overnight.

He began eating. First he just drank the juice, spoon after spoon. The warmth spread through his body, his insides greeted that skilly with a joyful fluttering. This was it! This was good! This was the brief moment for which a *zek* lives.

For a little while Shukhov forgot all his grievances, forgot that his sentence was long, that the day was long, that once again there would be no Sunday. For the moment he had only one thought: we shall survive. We shall survive it all. God willing, we'll see the end of it!

When he had supped up the hot juice from both bowls he emptied what was left in one into the other – tipping it up and then scraping it clean with his spoon. He would feel easier not having to think about the second bowl, not having to guard it with his eyes or his hand.

Now that his eyes were off duty he shot a glance at his neighbours' bowls. The man to his left had nothing but water. Dirty dogs – treating fellow *zeks* like that!

Now Shukhov was eating cabbage with the remains of his slop. The two bowls between them had caught a single potato – in Tsezar's bowl it was. A middling sort of potato, frost-bitten of course, sweetish and with hard bits in it. There was hardly any fish at all, just an occasional glimpse of a boiled-bare backbone. Still, every bone and every fin had to be thoroughly chewed, and the juice sucked out of them – the juice did you good. All this, of course, took time, but Shukhov was in no hurry. Today was a holiday for him: he'd lifted two portions for dinner and two for supper. Any other business could be put off while he dealt with this.

Though maybe he ought to call on the Latvian for his tobacco. There might be none left by morning.

Shukhov was eating his supper without bread: two portions with bread as well would be a bit too rich. The bread would come in useful tomorrow. The belly is an ungrateful wretch, it never remembers past favours, it always wants more tomorrow.

Shukhov finished off his skilly, not taking much notice of those around him – it didn't much matter, he was content with his lawful portion and had no hankering after anything more. All the same, he did notice the tall old man, Yu-81, sit down opposite him when the place became vacant. Shukhov knew that he belonged to Gang 64, and standing in line in the parcel room he'd heard that 64 had been sent to Sotsgorodok in place of 104, and spent the whole day stringing up barbed wire – making themselves a compound – with nowhere to get a warm.

He'd heard that this old man had been in prison time out of mind, in fact as long as the Soviet state had existed, that all the amnesties had passed him by, and that as soon as he finished one tenner they'd pinned another on him. This was Shukhov's chance to take a close look at him. With crookbacked old lags all round he was as straight as could be. He sat tall, as though he'd put something on the bench under him. That head hadn't needed a barber for ages: the life of luxury had caused all his hair to fall out. The old man's eyes didn't dart round at whatever was going on in the mess, but stared blindly at something over Shukhov's head. He was steadily eating his thin skilly, but instead of almost dipping his head in the bowl like the rest of them he carried his battered wooden spoon up high. He had no teeth left, upper or lower, but his bony gums chewed his bread just as well without them. His face was worn thin, but it wasn't the weak face of a burnt-out invalid, it was like dark chiselled stone. You could tell from his big chapped and blackened hands that in all his years inside he'd never had a soft job as a trusty. But he refused to knuckle under: he didn't put his three hundred grammes on a dirty table, splashed all over, like the others, he put it on a rag he washed regularly.

No time to go on studying him, though. Shukhov licked his spoon and tucked it inside his boot, crammed his cap on his head, rose, picked up the bread – his own ration and Tsezar's – and left. You went out by the back porch, past two orderlies with nothing to do except lift the catch, let you out, and lower the catch again.

Shukhov left with a well-filled belly, at peace with himself, and decided to pop over to the Latvian even though it was nearly lights out. He strode briskly towards Hut 7, without stopping to leave the bread at No. 9.

The moon was as high as it would ever be, it looked like a hole cut in the sky. The sky was cloudless. With here and there the brightest stars you ever saw. But Shukhov had less time still for studying the sky. All he knew was that the frost wasn't easing up. Somebody had heard from the free workers – it had been on the radio – that they were expecting thirty degrees below at night and forty by morning.

You could hear things a long way off. A tractor roaring in the settlement. The grating noise of an excavator over towards the highroad. The crunch of every pair of felt boots walking or running across the camp.

There was no wind now.

He was going to buy homegrown tobacco at the same price as before – a rouble for a tumblerful. Outside, that amount cost three roubles, or more, depending on quality. But prices in the camps weren't like those anywhere else. You weren't allowed to hang on to money, so what little you had bought more. This camp paid no money wage. (In Ust-Izhma Shukhov had earned thirty roubles a month – better than nothing.) If a man's family sent him money it wasn't passed on to him but credited to his personal account. This credit gave him the right to buy toilet soap, mouldy gingerbread and Prima cigarettes once a month in the camp shop. Whether you liked them or not you had to buy the goods once you'd ordered them through the commandant. If you didn't buy, the money was written off and you'd seen the last of it.

Money came Shukhov's way only from the private jobs he did: two roubles for making slippers from rags supplied by the customer, an agreed price for patching a jerkin.

Hut 7 wasn't divided into two large sections like No. 9. In Hut 7 ten doors opened onto a large corridor. Seven doubledecker bunks were wedged into every room, and occupied by a single gang. There was also a cubicle below the night-tub storeroom, and another for the hut monitor. The artists had a cubicle as well.

Shukhov went into the room where his Latvian was. He was lying on the lower bed space with his feet up on the brace, gabbling away to his neighbour in Latvian. Shukhov sat down by him, and mumbled some sort of greeting. The other man answered without lowering his feet. It was a small room, and they were all curious to know who this was and why he had come. Both of them realised this, so Shukhov sat there talking about nothing. How're you getting along, then? Not too bad. Cold today. Yes, it is.

He waited for the others to start talking again – they were arguing about the Korean war: would there be a world war now that the Chinese had joined in? – then bent his head towards the Latvian:

"Any homegrown?"

"Yes."

"Let's have a look."

The Latvian swung his feet down from the angle-brace, lowered them to the gangway and rose. A skinflint, this Latvian – frightened to death he might stuff one smoke too many into the tumbler.

He showed Shukhov the pouch and snapped open the clasp.

Shukhov took a pinch onto his palm and saw that it was the same as last time – same cut, and dark brown. He raised it to his nose and sniffed – yes, it was the same. But what he said to the Latvian was, "Doesn't seem the same somehow."

"It is! It is the same!" the Latvian said angrily. "I never have any other sort, it's always the same."

"All right, all right," Shukhov said agreeably. "Give me a good tumblerful and I'll try a puff. Maybe I'll take two lots."

He said give me a good tumblerful because the Latvian always packed the tobacco loosely.

The Latvian took another pouch fatter than the first from under his pillow and got a beaker from his locker. A plastic one, but Shukhov had measured it and knew it held the same as a glass tumbler.

The Latvian shook tobacco into it.

"Come on, press it down a bit," Shukhov said, pushing his own finger into the beaker.

"I don't need your help." The Latvian snatched the beaker away angrily and pressed the tobacco down himself, but less firmly. He shook in some more.

In the meantime Shukhov unbuttoned his jerkin and groped in the quilted lining for the bit of paper which only his fingers could feel. He used both hands to ease it gradually through the padding towards a little hole in quite a different part of the lining, loosely drawn together with two little stitches. When he had worked it as far as the hole he pulled the stitches out with his fingernails, folded the piece of paper lengthwise yet again (it was already folded into a long narrow strip) and drew it out. A two-rouble note. A well-worn one that didn't crackle.

Somebody in the room was bellowing: "Old Man Whiskers won't ever let you go! He wouldn't trust his own brother, let alone a bunch of cretins like you!"

The good thing about hard-labour camps is that you have all the freedom in the world to sound off. In Ust-Izhma you'd only have to whisper that people couldn't buy matches outside and they'd clap another ten on you. Here you could shout anything you liked from a top bunk and the stoolies wouldn't report it because the security officer couldn't care less.

But Shukhov couldn't afford to hang around talking.

"It's still pretty loose," he complained.

"Here, then!" the other man said, adding an extra pinch.

Shukhov took his pouch from his inside pocket and tipped the homegrown into it from the beaker.

"Right," he said. He didn't want to rush off with his first sweet cigarette on the go. "Fill me another."

He haggled a bit more while the beaker was filled again, then handed his two roubles over, nodded to the Latvian and went on his way.

Once outside he was in a great hurry to reach his own hut. He didn't want to miss Tsezar when he got back with the parcel.

But Tsezar was there already, sitting on his lower bunk, feasting his eyes. He had arranged what he'd brought on the bed and the locker. Both were screened from the lamp overhead by Shukhov's upper bunk, and it was pretty dark down there.

Shukhov bent over, inserted himself between Tsezar's bed space and the captain's and held his hand out.

"Your bread, Tsezar Markovich."

He didn't say, "You got it, then" – that would have been a hint that he was entitled to a share for keeping Tsezar's place in the queue. He knew his rights, of course. But even after eight years on general duties he was no scrounger, and as time went by he was more and more determined not to be.

He couldn't control his eyes, though – the hawk-eyes of an old camp hand. They skimmed over the contents of Tsezar's parcel laid out on the bed and the locker. The wrappings had not all been removed, and some bags had not been opened at all, but a quick glance and a sniff to make sure told Shukhov that Tsezar had been sent sausage, condensed milk, a big smoked fish, some fatback, biscuits with a nice smell, cake with a different nice smell, at least two kilos of lump sugar, and maybe some butter, as well as cigarettes, pipe tobacco, and quite a few other things.

He learnt all this in the time it took to say:

"Your bread, Tsezar Markovich."

Tsezar's eyes were wild and his hair all tousled. He was

drunk with excitement. (People who received parcels of groceries always got into that state.) He waved the bread away:

"Keep it, Ivan Denisovich."

The skilly, and two hundred grammes of bread as well – that was a full supper, worth quite as much as Shukhov's share of Tsezar's parcel.

He immediately stopped expecting anything from the goodies on display. No good letting your belly get excited when there's nothing to come.

He'd got four hundred grammes of bread, and another two hundred, and at least two hundred in his mattress. That was plenty. He could scoff two hundred now, gobble up five hundred and fifty in the morning, and still have four hundred to take to work. He was really living it up! The bread in the mattress could stay there a bit. Good job he'd stitched the hole up in time. Somebody in Gang 75 had had things pinched from his locker. (Ask the Supreme Soviet to look into it!)

Some people take the view that a man with a parcel is always a tightwad, you have to gouge what you can out of him. But when you think of it – it's easy come, easy go. Even those lucky people are sometimes glad to earn an extra bowl of gruel between parcels. Or scrounge a butt. A bit for the warder, a bit for the team foreman, and you can't leave out the trusty in the parcel room. If you do he'll mislay your parcel next time round and it'll be there a week before it gets on the list. Then there's the clerk in the storeroom, where all the groceries have to be handed in – Tsezar will be taking a bagful there before work parade next morning to be kept safe from thieves, and hut searches, and because the commandant has so ordered – if you don't make the clerk a handsome gift he'll pinch a bit here and a bit there . . . He sits there all day behind a locked door with other men's groceries, the rat, and there's no way of checking up on him. Then there's payment for services rendered (by Shukhov to Tsezar, for instance). Then there'll be a little something for the bath-house man, so he'll pick you out a decent set of clean underwear. Then there's the barber, who shaves you "with paper" – wiping the razor on a scrap of paper, not your bare knee – it may not amount to much, but you have to give him three or four cigarettes. Then there'll be somebody in the CES – to make sure your letters are put aside separately and not lost in the ruck. Then supposing you want to dodge work and lie up for a day in the compound – you need to fix the doctor. You're bound to give something to your neighbour who eats from the same locker-top, like the captain does with Tsezar. He counts every bite you take. The most shameless *zek* can't hold out against that.

So those who always think the other man's radish is plumper than their own might feel envy, but Shukhov knew what was what and didn't let his belly rumble for other people's goodies.

By now he'd pulled his boots off, climbed up on his bunk, taken the fragment of steel out of his mitten, examined it, and made up his mind to look for a good stone next day and hone himself a cobbler's knife – work at it a bit morning and evening and in four days he'd have a great little knife with a sharp curved blade.

For the time being, the steel had to be hidden, even at night. He could wedge it between his bedboards and one of the crossbars. While the captain wasn't there for the dust to fall in his face, Shukhov turned back his heavy mattress (stuffed with sawdust, not shavings) at the pillow end, and set about hiding the blade.

His neighbours up top – Alyoshka the Baptist and the two Estonian brothers on the next bunk across the gangway – could see him, but Shukhov knew he was safe with them.

Fetyukov passed down the hut sobbing. He was bent double. His lips were smeared with blood. He must have been beaten up again for licking out dishes. He walked past the whole team without looking at anybody, not trying to hide his tears, climbed onto his bunk, and buried his head in his mattress.

You felt sorry for him really. He wouldn't see his time out. He didn't know how to look after himself.

At that point the captain appeared, looking happy, carrying specially brewed tea in a mess tin. There were two buckets of tea in the hut, if you could call it tea. Warm and tea-coloured, all right, but like washing-up water. And the bucket made it smell of mouldy wood pulp. Tea for the common working man, that was. Buynovsky must have got a handful of real tea from Tsezar, popped it in the mess tin and toddled off to the boiler. He settled down at his locker, mighty pleased with himself.

"Nearly scalded my fingers under the tap," he said, showing off.

Down below there Tsezar unfolded a sheet of paper and laid things out on it. Shukhov put his mattress back in place so he wouldn't see and get upset. But yet again they couldn't manage without him. Tsezar rose to his full height in the gangway, so that his eyes were on a level with Shukhov's, and winked:

"Denisovich! Lend us your ten-day gadget."

The little folding knife he meant. Shukhov had one hidden in his bed. Smaller than your finger crooked at the middle knuckle, but the devil would cut fatback five fingers thick. Shukhov had made a beautiful job of that knife and kept it well honed.

He felt for the knife, drew it out and handed it over. Tsezar gave him a nod and vanished again.

The knife was another earner. Because you could land in the hole (ten days!) for keeping it. Only somebody with no conscience at all would say lend us your knife so we can cut our sausage, and don't think you're getting any.

Tsezar had put himself in debt to Shukhov again.

Now that he'd dealt with the bread and the knives Shukhov fished out his pouch. He took from it a pinch exactly as big as that he had borrowed and held it out across the gangway to the Estonian, with a thank you.

The Estonian's lips straightened into a smile of sorts, he muttered something to his brother, and they rolled a separate cigarette to sample Shukhov's tobacco.

Go ahead and try it, it's no worse than yours! Shukhov would have tried it himself, but the clock in his guts said it was very close to roll-call. Just the time for the warders to come prowling round the huts. If he wanted a smoke he'd have to go out in the corridor quick, and he fancied it was a bit warmer up on his top bunk. It wasn't at all warm in the hut, and the ceiling was still patterned with hoar frost. It would be a shivery night, but for the time being it was just about bearable.

All his little jobs done, Shukhov began breaking bits from his two hundred grammes. He couldn't help listening to the captain and Tsezar drinking tea and talking down below.

"Help yourself, Captain, don't be shy! Have some of this smoked fish. Have some sausage."

"Thank you, I will."

"Butter yourself a piece of this loaf! It's a real Moscow baton!"

"Dear-oh-dear-oh-dear, I just can't believe that some-where or other batons are still being baked. This sudden abundance reminds me of something that once happened to me. It was at Sevastopol, before the Yalta Conference. The town was absolutely starving and we had to show an American admiral round. So they set up a shop specially, chockful of foodstuffs, but it wasn't to be opened until they saw us half a block away, so that the locals wouldn't have time to crowd the place out. Even so, the shop was half-full one minute after it opened. And you couldn't ask for the wrong thing. 'Look, butter!' people were shout-ing, 'real butter! And white bread!' "

Two hundred harsh voices were raising a din in their half of the hut, but Shukhov still thought he could make out the clang of hammer on rail. Nobody else heard, though. Shukhov also noticed that the warder they called Snub-nose – a short, red-faced young man – had appeared in the hut. He was holding a piece of paper, and this and his whole manner showed that he hadn't come to catch people smoking or drive them outside for roll-call, but was looking for somebody in particular.

Snub-nose consulted his piece of paper and asked:

"Where's one-o-four?"

"Here," they answered. The Estonians concealed their cigarette and waved the smoke away.

"Where's the foreman?"

"What d'you want?" Tyurin spoke from his bed, swinging his legs over the edge so that his feet barely touched the floor.

"Have the men who were told to submit written explanations got them ready?"

"They're doing it," Tyurin said confidently.

"They should have been in by now."

"Some of my men are more or less illiterate, it's hard work for them." (Tsezar and the captain he was talking about. He was a lad, was Tyurin. Never stuck for an answer.) "We've got no pens, nor ink."

"Well you should have."

"They keep confiscating it."

"Watch it, foreman, just mind what you're saying, or I'll have you in the cell-block," Snub-nose promised, mildly. "The explanatory notes will be in the warders' barracks before work parade in the morning! And you will report that all prohibited articles have been handed in to the personal property store. Understood?"

"Understood."

("The captain's in the clear!" Shukhov thought. The captain himself was purring over his sausage and didn't hear a thing.)

"Now, then," said the warder. "Shcha-301 – is he in your gang?"

"I'll have to look at the list," the foreman said, pretending ignorance. "How can anybody be expected to remember these blasted numbers?" (If he could drag it out till roll-call he might save Buynovsky at least for the night.)

"Buynovsky – is he here?"

"Eh? That's me!" the captain piped up from his hiding place under Shukhov's top bunk.

The quick louse is always first on the comb.

"You, is it? Right then, Shcha-301. Get ready."

"To go where?"

"You know where."

The captain only sighed and groaned. Taking a squadron of torpedo-boats out into a stormy sea in the pitch dark must have been easier for him than leaving his friends' company for the icy cell-block.

"How many days?" he asked in a faint voice.

"Ten. Come along now, hurry it up!"

Just then the orderlies began yelling "Roll-call! Everybody out for roll-call!"

The warder sent to call the roll must be in the hut already.

The captain looked back, wondering whether to take his overcoat. If he did, though, they'd whip it off him and leave him just his jerkin. So better go as he was. The captain had hoped for a while that Volkovoy would forget – but Volkovoy never forgot or forgave – and had made no preparations, hadn't even hidden himself a bit of tobacco in his jerkin. No good holding it in his hand – they'd take it off him the moment they frisked him.

All the same, Tsezar slipped him a couple of cigarettes while he was putting his cap on.

"Well, so long chums," the captain said with a miserable look, nodding to his team-mates, and followed the warder out of the hut. Several voices called after him, "Keep smiling," "Don't let them get you down" – but there was nothing much you could say. Gang 104 had built the punishment block themselves and knew all about it: the walls were of stone, the floor cement, there were no windows at all, the stove was kept just warm enough for the ice on the wall to melt and form puddles on the floor. You slept on bare boards, got three hundred grammes of bread a day, skilly only every third day.

Ten days! Ten days in that cell-block if they were strict about it and made you sit out the whole stint meant your health was ruined for life. It meant tuberculosis and the rest of your days in hospital.

Fifteen days in there and you'd be six feet under.

Thank Heaven for your cosy hut, and keep your nose clean.

"Outside, I said – I'll count to three," the hut orderly shouted. "If anybody's not outside when I get to three I'll take his number and report him to the warder."

The hut orderly's another arch-bastard. Imagine – they lock him in with us for the whole night and he isn't afraid of anybody because he's got the camp brass behind him. It's the other way round – everybody's afraid of him. He'll either betray you to the warders or punch you in the kisser. Disabled, supposed to be, because he lost a finger in a brawl, but he looks like a hood. And that's just what he is – convicted as a common criminal, but they pinned a charge under Article 58 Subsection 14★ on him as well, which is why he landed in this camp.

There was nothing to stop him jotting your name down, handing it to the warder and it was two days in the hole, normal working hours. Men had been drifting towards the door, but now they all crowded out, those on the top bunks flopping down like bears to join the milling crowd, trying to push their way through the narrow opening. Shukhov sprang down nimbly, holding the cigarette he'd just rolled and had been wanting so long, thrust his feet into his boots and was ready to go – but he took pity on Tsezar. Not that he wanted to earn a bit more from Tsezar, he just pitied the man with all his heart: Tsezar might think a lot of himself, but he didn't know the first thing about the facts of life. When you got a parcel you didn't sit gloating over it, you rushed it off to the storeroom before roll-call. Eating could wait. But what could Tsezar do with his parcel now? If he turned out for roll-call carrying that great big bag what a laugh

★ "Counter-revolutionary sabotage", a charge applicable to any action judged to damage the economy that would be – five hundred men would be roaring with laughter. If he left the stuff where it was it would very likely be pinched by the first man back from roll-call. (In Ust-Izhma the system was even tougher: the crooks would always be home from work first and by the time the others got in their lockers would be cleaned out.)

Shukhov saw Tsezar flapping – but he should have thought about it sooner. He was shoving the fatback and sausage under his shirt – if nothing else he might be able to take them out to roll-call and save them.

Shukhov took pity on him and told him how it was done:

"Sit tight, Tsezar Markovich – lie low, out of the light and go out last. Don't stir till the warder and the orderlies come round the beds looking in every nook and cranny – then you can go out. Tell 'em you aren't well! And I'll go out first and hop back in first. That's the way to do it."

And off he dashed.

He had to be pretty rough to start with, shoving his way through the crowd (taking good care, though, of the cigarette in his clenched hand). But there was no shoving in the corridor shared by both halves of the hut and near the outer door. The crafty lot stuck like flies to the walls leaving free passage for one at a time between the ranks: go out in the cold if you're stupid enough, we'll hang on here a bit! We've been freezing outside all day as it is, why freeze for an extra ten minutes now? We aren't that stupid, you know. You peg out today – I'll wait till tomorrow!

Any other time Shukhov would have propped himself up against the wall with the rest. But now he strode by sneering. "What are you afraid of, never seen a Siberian frost before? The wolves are out sunbathing – come and try it! Give us a light, old chap!"

He lit up just inside the door and went out onto the

porch. "Wolf's sunshine" was what they jokingly called the moonlight where Shukhov came from.

The moon was very high now. As far again and it would be at its highest. Sky white with a greenish tinge, stars bright but far between. Snow sparkling white, barrack walls also white. Lamps might as well not be there.

The black crowd was growing thicker outside the next hut. They were coming out to line up. And outside that other one. From hut to hut the buzz of conversation was almost drowned by the crunch of snow under boots.

Five men went down the steps and lined up facing the door. Three others followed them. Shukhov took his place in the second rank with those three. After a munch of bread and with a cig in his mouth it wasn't too bad standing there. The Latvian hadn't cheated him — it was really good tobacco, heady and sweet-smelling. Men gradually trickled through the door, and by now there were two or three more ranks of five behind Shukhov. Those already out were in a foul temper. What did the lousy bastards think they were doing, hanging round in the corridor instead of coming outside? Leaving us to freeze.

No *zek* ever lays eyes on a clock or watch. What good would it do him anyway? All a *zek* needs to know is — how soon is reveille? How long till work parade? Till dinner-time? Till lights out?

Anyway, evening roll-call is supposed to be at nine. But that's not the end of it, because they can make you go through the whole rigmarole twice or three times over. You can't get to sleep before ten. And reveille, they reckon, is at five. Small wonder that the Moldavian fell asleep just now before knocking-off time. If a *zek* manages to get warm he's asleep right away. By the end of the week there's so much lost sleep to make up for that if you aren't bundled out to work on Sunday the hut is one great heap of sleeping bodies.

Aha – *zeks* were pouring down from the porch now – the warder and the hut orderly were kicking their behinds. Give it to them, the swine!

"What the hell are you playing at up there?" the front ranks yelled at them. "Skimming the cream from shit? If you'd come out sooner they'd have finished counting long ago."

The whole hut came tumbling out. Four hundred men – eighty ranks of five. They queued up – neat fives to begin with, then higgledy-piggledy.

"Sort yourselves out at the back there!" the hut orderly roared from the steps.

Like hell they would, the bastards!

Tsezar came out hunched up, acting the invalid, followed by two orderlies from the other half of the hut, two from Shukhov's and another man with a limp. These five became the front rank, so that Shukhov was now in the third. Tsezar was packed off to the rear.

After this the warder came out onto the porch. "Form up in fives," he shouted at the rear ranks. He had a good pair of tonsils. "Form up in fives," the hut orderly bellowed. His tonsils were even healthier.

Still they don't move, damn their eyes.

The hut orderly shot down the steps, hurled himself at them, cursing and thumping backs. He took care which backs he thumped, though. Only the meek were lambasted.

They finally lined up properly. He went back to his place, and shouted with the warder:

"First five! Second! Third!"

Each five shot off into the hut as its number was called. Finished for the day.

Unless there's a second roll-call, that is. Any herdsman can count better than those layabouts. He may not be able to read, but the whole time he's driving his herd he knows whether all his calves are there or not. This lot are supposed to be trained, but it's done them no good.

The winter before, there'd been no drying rooms in the camp and everybody kept his boots in the barracks overnight – so they'd turfed everybody out for a second, a third, or even a fourth count. The men didn't even dress, but rolled out wrapped in their blankets. Since then drying rooms had been built – not for every hut, but each gang got a chance to dry its boots every third day. So now they'd started doing second counts inside the huts: driving the men from one half to the other.

Shukhov wasn't first in, but he ran without taking his eyes off the one man in front. He hurried to Tsezar's bed, sat on it, and tugged his boots off. Then he climbed up onto a handy bunk and stood his boots on the stove to dry. You just had to get in first. Then back to Tsezar's bed. He sat with his legs tucked under him, one eye watching to see that Tsezar's sack wasn't whipped from under his pillow, the other on the look-out for anybody storming the stove and knocking his boots off their perch.

He had to shout at one man. "Hey! You there, Ginger! Want a boot in your ugly mug? Put your own boots up, but don't touch other people's!"

Zeks were pouring into the hut now. In Gang 20 somebody was shouting "Hand over your boots!" The men taking the boots to the drying room would be let out and the door locked behind them. They'd come running back shouting: "Citizen warder! Let us in!"

Meanwhile the warders would gather in the HQ hut with their boards to check their book-keeping and see whether anyone had escaped.

None of that mattered to Shukhov at present. Ah – here comes Tsezar, diving between the bunks on his way home.

"Thanks, Ivan Denisovich."

Shukhov nodded and scrambled up top like a squirrel. He could finish eating his two hundred grammes, he could smoke a second cigarette, or he could just go to sleep.

Only he was in such high spirits after such a good day he didn't really feel much like sleeping.

Making his bed wasn't much of a job: he just whisked off his blackish blanket, lay down on the mattress (he couldn't have slept on a sheet since he'd left home in '41, in fact he couldn't for the life of him see why women bothered with sheets, it just made extra washing), laid his head on the pillow stuffed with shavings, shoved his feet into his jerkin, spread his jacket over his blanket and –

"Thanks be to thee, O God, another day over!"

He was thankful that he wasn't sleeping in the punishment cell. Here it was just about bearable.

Shukhov lay with his head towards the window, Alyoshka on the other half of the bunk with his head at the other end, where light from the bulb would reach him. He was reading his Testament again.

The lamp wasn't all that far away. They could read or even sew.

Alyoshka heard Shukhov thank God out loud, and looked round.

"There you are, Ivan Denisovich, your soul is asking to be allowed to pray to God. Why not let it have its way, eh?"

Shukhov shot a glance at him: the light in his eyes was like candle-flame. Shukhov sighed.

"Because, Alyoshka, prayers are like petitions – either they don't get through at all, or else it's 'complaint rejected'."

Four sealed boxes stood in front of the staff hut, and were emptied once a month by someone delegated for that purpose. Many prisoners dropped petitions into those boxes, then waited, counting the days, expecting an answer in two months, one month...

There would be no answer. Or else – "complaint rejected".

"That's because you never prayed long enough or fervently enough, that's why your prayers weren't answered. Prayer must be persistent. And if you have faith and say to a mountain, make way, it will make way."

Shukhov grinned, rolled himself another cigarette, and got a light from the Estonian.

"Don't talk rot, Alyoshka. I never saw mountains going anywhere. Come to that I've never seen any mountains. But when you and your whole Baptist club did all that praying in the Caucasus did one single mountain ever move over?"

Poor devils. What harm does their praying do anybody? Collected twenty-five years all round. That's how things are nowadays: twenty-five is the only size in sentences.

"We didn't pray for anything like that, Denisovich," Alyoshka said earnestly. He moved round with his Testament until he was almost face to face with Shukhov. "The Lord's behest was that we should pray for no earthly or transient thing except our daily bread. 'Give us this day our daily bread'."

"Our ration, you mean?" Shukhov asked.

Alyoshka went on undeterred, exhorting Shukhov

with his eyes more than his words, patting and stroking his hand.

"Ivan Denisovich! We shouldn't pray for somebody to send us a parcel, or for an extra portion of skilly. What people prize highly is vile in the sight of God! We must pray for spiritual things, asking God to remove the scum of evil from our hearts."

"No, you listen to me. There's a priest at our church in Polomnya . . ."

"Don't tell me about your priest!" Alyoshka begged, his brow creased with pain.

"No, you just listen." Shukhov raised himself on his elbow. "In our parish, Polomnya, nobody was better off than the priest. If we got a roofing job, say, we charged other people thirty-five a day but him we charged a hundred. And there was never a peep out of him. He was paying alimony to three women in three different towns and living with his fourth family. The local bishop was under his thumb, our priest greased his palm well. If they sent any other priest along, ours would make his life hell, he wasn't going to share with anybody."

"Why are you telling me about this priest? The Orthodox Church has turned its back on the Gospels – *they* don't get put inside or else they get off with five years because their faith is not firm."

Shukhov calmly observed Alyoshka's agitation, puffing on his cigarette.

"Look, Alyoshka" – smoke got into the Baptist's eyes as Shukhov pushed his outstretched hand aside. "I'm not against God, see. I'm quite ready to believe in God. But I just don't believe in heaven and hell. Why do you think everybody deserves either heaven or hell? What sort of idiots do you take us for? That's what I don't like."

Shukhov lay back again, after carefully dropping his ash into the space behind his head, between the bunk and the window, so as not to burn the captain's belongings. Lost in thought, he no longer heard Alyoshka's muttering.

"Anyway," he concluded, "pray as much as you like, they won't knock anything off your sentence. You'll serve your time from bell to bell whatever happens."

Alyoshka was horrified. "That's just the sort of thing you shouldn't pray for! What good is freedom to you? If you're free your faith will soon be choked by thorns! Be glad you're in prison. Here you have time to think about your soul. Remember what the Apostle Paul says: 'What are you doing, weeping and breaking my heart? For I am ready not only to be imprisoned but even to die in Jerusalem for the name of the Lord Jesus.'*"

Shukhov stared at the ceiling and said nothing. He no longer knew whether he wanted to be free or not. To begin with he'd wanted it very much, and totted up every evening how many days he still had to serve. Then he'd got fed up with it. And still later it had gradually dawned on him that people like himself were not allowed to go home but packed off into exile. And there was no knowing where the living was easier – here or there.

The one thing he might want to ask God for was to let him go home.

But they wouldn't let him go home.

Alyoshka wasn't lying though. You could tell from his voice and his eyes that he was glad to be in prison.

"Look, Alyoshka," Shukhov explained, "it's worked out pretty well for you. Christ told you to go to jail, and you did it, for Christ. But what am I here for? Because they weren't ready for the war in '41 – is that the reason?

*Acts 21, 13

Was that my fault?"

"No second roll-call by the look of it," Kildigs growled from his bed. He yawned.

"Wonders will never cease," Shukhov said. "Maybe we can get some sleep."

At that very minute, just as the hut was growing quiet, they heard the rattle of a bolt at the outer door of the hut. The two men who'd taken the boots to be dried dashed into the hut shouting "Second roll-call!"

A warder followed them, shouting "Out into the other half!"

Some of them were already sleeping! They all bestirred themselves, grumbling and groaning as they drew their boots on (very few of them were in their underpants, they mostly slept as they were, in their padded trousers – without them your feet would be frozen stiff even under a blanket).

Shukhov swore loudly. "Damn them to hell!" But he wasn't all that angry, because he hadn't fallen asleep yet.

Tsezar's hand reached up to place two biscuits, two lumps of sugar, and one round chunk of sausage on Shukhov's bed.

"Thank you Tsezar Markovich," Shukhov said, lowering his head into the gangway between bunks. "Better give me your bag to put under my pillow for safety." (A passing *zek's* thieving hands wouldn't find it so quickly up there – and anyway, who would expect Shukhov to have anything?)

Tsezar passed his tightly tied white bag up to Shukhov. Shukhov tucked it under his mattress and was going to wait a bit until more men had been herded out so that he wouldn't have to stand barefoot on the corridor floor so long. But the warder snarled at him –

"You over there! In the corner!"

So Shukhov sprang to the floor, landing lightly on his bare feet (his boots and footrags were so cosy up there on the stove it would be a pity to move them). He had cobbled so many pairs of slippers – but always for others, never for himself. Still, he was used to it and it wouldn't be for long.

Slippers were confiscated if found in the daytime.

The gangs who'd handed in their boots for drying were all right now if they had slippers, but some had only footrags tied round their feet, and others were barefoot.

"Get on with it! Get on with it!" the warder roared. The hut orderly joined in: "Want a bit of stick, you scum?"

Most of them were crammed into the other half of the hut, and the last out, Shukhov for one, into the corridor. He stood against the partition wall by the night bucket. The floor was damp to his feet, and an icy draught blew along it from the lobby. Everybody was out now but the warder and the hut orderly went to look yet again whether anybody was hiding, or curled up asleep in a dark spot. Too few or too many at the count meant trouble – yet another re-check. The two of them went round and round, then came back to the door.

One by one, but quickly now, they were allowed back in. Shukhov squeezed in eighteenth, dashed to his bunk, hoisted his foot into a bracket and – heave-ho! – up he went. Great. Feet into jerkin sleeve again, blanket on top, jacket over that and we're asleep! The whole lot in the other half of the barracks would now be herded into this half – but that was their bad luck.

Tsezar came back. Shukhov lowered the bag to him.

Now Alyoshka was back. He had no sense at all, Alyoshka, never earned a thing, but did favours for everybody.

"Here you are, Alyoshka!" Shukhov handed him one biscuit.

Alyoshka was all smiles. "Thank you! You won't have any for yourself!"

"Eat it!"

If we're without, we can always earn something.

He himself took the lump of sausage – and popped it into his mouth. Get the teeth to it. Chew, chew, chew! Lovely meaty smell! Meat juice, the real thing. Down it went, into his belly.

End of sausage.

The other stuff he planned to eat before work parade.

He covered his head with the skimpy, grubby blanket and stopped listening to the *zeks* from the other half crowding in between the bunks to be counted.

Shukhov felt pleased with life as he went to sleep. A lot of good things had happened that day. He hadn't been thrown in the hole. The gang hadn't been dragged off to Sotsgorodok. He'd swiped the extra gruel at dinner-time. The foreman had got a good rate for the job. He'd enjoyed working on the wall. He hadn't been caught with the blade at the searchpoint. He'd earned a bit from Tsezar that evening. And he'd bought his tobacco.

The end of an unclouded day. Almost a happy one.

Just one of the three thousand six hundred and fifty-three days of his sentence, from bell to bell.

The extra three were for leap years.

1959